EVER DARK

THE VAMPIRE KING RETURNS (BOOK 2)

EVER DARK

BOOK TWO

❧

X. ARATARE

R

INTRODUCTION

Julian Harrow and Christian Thorne are now Vampires! And both young men have been united with their Masters after trials and tribulations. But if they thought that becoming Vampires was dangerous and exciting, being the fledglings of the exiled Lord Balthazar Ravenscroft and the Vampire King Daemon will blow that out of the water. Because both Balthazar and Daemon have enemies that are intent on making sure that they and their new fledglings are given their Second Deaths.

AWKWARD MOMENTS

"*Y*ou know, the next time I'm in trouble I *won't* be calling you, Arcius," Vampire Lord Balthazar Ravenscroft said waspishly to the hulking Berserker Vampire Confessor Arcius Kane.

In Christian Thorn's eyes Arcius looked more like a cuddly bear at the moment, all sheepish movements and downcast eyes. Clearly, the Confessor was slightly embarrassed by falling to his knees after seeing Daemon. Thinking of the hundreds of wolves breaking through the glass barrier, Christian had to admit that Daemon *was* impressive.

And other things.

Sheepish yet calm, Arcius answered, "You didn't call for me. I just came. And you were *fine*. He had stopped choking you by the time I had come in."

"My neck is bruised and my throat is sore." Balthazar pointed to his throat.

Personally, Christian didn't see anything wrong with Balthazar's neck. It had been turning red and purple immediately after Daemon had released Balthazar from his death grip, but now it was perfectly fine. He found it mildly amusing that this very tough Vampire Lord was acting like a drama queen.

1

"Listen to my voice!" Balthazar cried. "It's raspy from ill use by that–that–"

"*King?*" Arcius supplied helpfully.

Balthazar though was having none of that. "That *bastard* is responsible."

The Confessor shook his head and clucked softly. "Careful, Balthazar, he might hear you and pin you to the wall again."

"He was made of *wolves*," Balthazar whined. "Not just one wolf. *Hundreds*. He breached my bedroom! Like some kind of–of–"

"*King?*" Arcius offered again even as he smiled indulgently at Balthazar. The Confessor hadn't seemed a dour fellow before Daemon arrived, but there was almost this giddy happiness to him now. Balthazar gave him a black look. In return, Arcius said, "Your bedroom wall is quite repaired. No sign of the gateway to the Ever Dark at all."

"A gateway would have been useful! But no, it's just a wall again!" Balthazar's hands rose up and down rather like the wings of a bird as it flapped on a line. "And *who* can do that exactly? Just–just *create* a new gateway between the two universes? Who–Don't say it! I *know* what you're going to say! A *king*."

"Not *a* king, Balthazar. *The* king. *Our* king," the Confessor corrected mildly.

"And he's taken over my bedroom!" Balthazar sounded really wounded now. "Kicked me out of my own space and–"

"Where else should our *king* stay, but in the best bedroom in the house?" Again, Arcius was mild as milk.

After Julian Harrow and Arcius had carried an unconscious Daemon to Balthazar's magnificent bed, Sophia Strange had rushed out to bring in Maddie the healer. Sophia had then surprisingly disappeared even as Maddie froze in shock at seeing Daemon. But then the healer came back to herself and burst into action. She immediately had attached an IV line to Daemon's arm and brought in half a dozen bags of blood to be dripped into his system.

"I've never worked on an Immortal before," Maddie had said nervously. Her gaze swept over the Vampire King who lay–magnificently in all his black leather and white fur–in the middle of Balthazar's bed looking ... well, looking like a *king.* "But I believe he will be fine with blood and rest."

"He was too weak to leave Ever Dark. He came here for me. Idiot," Julian breathed the last with an affectionate smile.

Julian had been sitting on the bed, holding one of the Vampire King's hands in his. He was looking at Daemon's peaceful face while biting his lower lip. Daemon's eyelids were closed, hiding those blood red irises.

"He didn't want Balthazar to feed you," Christian had said as he had moved nearer Julian.

Balthazar had stood frozen by Arcius at the door. The Vampire Lord had been fingering his throat and staring at Daemon with a mixture of shock and resentment.

"Yeah, that was the long and short of it. Guess he does want me as his fledgling after all. Or, at least, he doesn't want anyone else to have me," Julian answered, without looking away from Daemon's sleeping visage.

"He's beautiful," Christian said quietly.

Christian needed to know what his best friend felt towards this *alien* being. Though Daemon looked like a human—or rather a Vampire—those red eyes had shown that he wasn't. But there were other things about him—setting aside utterly the fact that he could become hundreds of wolves—that made Christian keenly aware that Daemon was not like everyone else. He worried a little as he saw some of that difference in Julian, though he could not put his finger on what it was.

"He is," Julian answered. A pause then, "And stubborn. And high-handed. And possessive. And–"

"You're worried about him," Christian interrupted gently.

Julian turned anguished eyes upon Christian. "If I hadn't agreed to feed from Balthazar, he wouldn't have done this! He may have put himself at risk by coming here this soon, Christian!"

"You didn't know, Julian." Christian laid a hand on Julian's arm comfortingly. "He wasn't communicating–"

"He was! I just couldn't hear him! He was frantic." Julian shook his head. "If he's damaged because of this—"

"I truly think he will be all right," Maddie said. She'd been quietly replacing an empty bag of blood with a fresh one as they had talked. The blood had practically been sucked into Daemon's veins.

"But nobody really knows, do they? He's one of a kind," Julian murmured.

Christian thought of the white hot hatred that had fueled his best friend for a decade against Vampires. Yet he shouldn't have been surprised that Julian would find it in his heart to care for one of them. It was easy to hate a group until one met individuals within that group that didn't match one's low expectations.

"He didn't show half as much concern for you when he sent you back to Earth on your own," Balthazar growled. His arms were crossed over his chest and he was glaring daggers at Daemon.

Arcius grasped his shoulder. His voice low, "Balthazar, please, let this go. Julian was never yours to begin with. You must accept this"

Balthazar shrugged off his hand and stormed out of the room with more muttered curses. The Confessor took a deep breath.

"Christian, Balthazar needs you right now." Arcius gestured for Christian to go with him after the Vampire Lord.

Christian was about to argue that Julian needed him *more*. Balthazar was acting out of pique in his opinion while Julian was really hurting. But his best friend cut off that argument.

"I'll be fine, Christian," Julian told him "Go on. Balthazar's been pretty banged up tonight. He was trying to do the right thing and no one is thanking him for it."

Still Christian had hesitated a moment. He hadn't been keen to leave his best friend at all with this strange Vampire that didn't speak out loud, but only through his mind and to Julian alone. The conversation while he'd pinned Balthazar to the wall had been one-sided. They'd only been able to hear Julian's responses, none of what Daemon had said. And then there were those red eyes. They glowed like hellfire. When Christian had met the Vampire King's gaze for a moment, he'd seen *something*.

A glimpse of eternity.

"If you're sure. I can come back immediately," Christian finally had said.

"I'm good. I'm just going to sit with him for a while. Need to know he's okay," Julian had answered.

So he'd reluctantly nodded and left the room after Arcius. They had found Balthazar on the first floor in a beautiful and airy living room. A fire crackled in the grate of a fireplace that bisected the large arched space. The myriad of reds, golds and whites in the flames fascinated Christian with his enhanced Vampiric vision. There were large, inviting sofas in white, dark blankets thrown over their backs that bracketed the area before the fireplace. Christian could already imagine curling down to read some historical treatise in order to prepare for one of his and Julian's shows.

If we're allowed to do that any longer.

He glanced over at Balthazar. The Vampire Lord was still going on about his "grievances". Despite what Arcius had said it didn't seem like Balthazar needed him at all. He was surprised that he was slightly miffed by it.

"He's not a guest! He barged in just when... when we were... when I was... Julian and Christian!" The Vampire Lord seemed unable to complete that sentence though. He strode angrily over to the roaring fireplace, resting one hand against the marble mantle piece while staring into the flames.

"It's good he came when he did," Christian spoke for the first time since they'd left Balthazar's bedroom. "If you'd fed Julian, I don't imagine he would have given Julian time to convince him not to kill you otherwise."

"I was doing what was *best*." Balthazar had been insisting on this since the whole strangling thing.

Arcius and Christian's gazes met for a moment, and, Christian felt he might have met a kindred spirit. The Confessor clearly believed that Balthazar–for all his good and true reasons–wasn't being one hundred percent honest with himself. He'd wanted Julian and Christian for himself. Any other reasoning he gave for why Julian needed

5

to drink from him, while it might have been correct, was *not* the deep root reason for his desire.

"Like Christian, I dread to think of what he would have done if you *had* fed Julian. The whole House might have been forfeit," Arcius pointed out.

"He would have to be blackhearted and unworthy of our fealty if he did that." Balthazar looked coldly furious.

Christian already knew that the Vampire Lord had a large problem with authority figures.

Considering what his Master did to him and the others, that was a good trait to have. But against Daemon? Yeah, the king fainted, but once he's truly himself again? I fear what he'll be able to do.

"He is our *king*. He has certain expectations of us. Trying to take his fledgling probably rises to the level of traitor in his mind," Arcius explained incredibly calmly. He'd said as much half a dozen times already. "He spared you when he could have killed you without a thought. Tell me you wouldn't have done the same and you're *not* a king."

"Julian's the only reason you're alive," Christian pointed out.

"I know. He's a dear boy. A very dear boy. That makes sense as he is *your* best friend. But Julian was–is–starving," Balthazar muttered. "It's not like Daemon can feed him yet."

"He tried to drink the bagged blood before. Maybe he'll try again. I'm actually pretty sure he will, considering how worried he is about Daemon," Christian said.

Balthazar merely nodded. Christian could see he was still sorely disappointed at not having "best friends" in his House. Christian was trying not to think about what this meant for him and Julian. He knew that Julian would not allow them to be parted. Neither would he. Balthazar and Daemon would have to learn to get along.

Or we'll dump both of them and go our own way.

His stomach twinged. He was starving. And, as if Balthazar felt it, too, the Vampire Lord swung around to face him. His brows bunched together and his mouth flattened as he took in Christian.

"You are hungry, and here I am, your Master, being incredibly thoughtless." Balthazar approached him and touched his biceps with both hands, holding him lightly.

Christian tensed, but forced himself to relax. He knew that Balthazar had noticed and there were the faintest lines of disappointment on his forehead.

"It's not you," Christian blurted out then gritted his teeth. He owed this man no real explanation for his reaction. Was it normal to be fine with strangers touching you? Shouldn't it be especially okay for good looking ones like Balthazar to do it? Even more especially, ones who had saved you and your best friend's lives? So Christian added, "I just am not good with people touching me that I don't know very well. But you seem... like a toucher."

Balthazar cocked his head to the side and gave Christian a fond smile. He squeezed his arms once and released them. "I am, but I don't want to breach your boundaries."

"You already have," Christian admitted, but then when he saw the crestfallen look on Balthazar's face, he quickly added, "But it's fine. I mean... It will be fine. Once I get to know you."

Considering we are bound together forever.

"We'll take it slow," Balthazar offered as he brightened. This was the first time he'd looked happy since Daemon had arrived.

"Okay. Maybe you can start by telling me about yourself." Christian knew nothing of the Vampire Lord.

Balthazar brightened. "Excellent, because I love talking about myself."

Arcius smirked. "At least, he's honest about that."

Balthazar scowled at the Confessor, but it quickly became a lopsided grin. "No one would believe me if I said anything else!"

"Why do you not take Christian to the guest house?" Arcius offered. "You need to feed to recover from your *grevious* wounds before feeding Christian. And I'm sure that Christian would benefit in understanding how this part of the House works."

"I'm sure that Daemon will need some humans to volunteer to feed him once he wakes, too," Balthazar said, his mouth flattening despite his obvious intention to play a good host.

"He is our king, Balthazar," Arcius said quietly. "I will have another room prepared for you for right now until he can be moved."

"Thank you, old friend. I do appreciate all you do even when you fall down on the job." Balthazar grinned.

Arcius just shook his head. "You will never let me live that down, will you?"

"Never," Balthazar replied cheerily.

Arcius grunted in amusement. Christian found himself grinning. He liked the way they were together. It seemed almost human.

"Also, let me know when his highness awakes," Balthazar requested dryly.

"I know you're not keen on Daemon, but I believe you should rethink that," Christian said.

"And why is that?" One of Balthazar's eyebrows lifted. "Don't tell me that you're a royal worshiper, too?"

"God, no." Christian almost violently shook his head. "I cannot think of a stupider way of governing than by bloodline."

"See, Arcius? Christian has a good head on his shoulders. He's *logical* and *scientific* in his thinking," Balthazar crowed at the Confessor.

"But since that *is* your way of government," Christian broke in, which had Arcius grinning back at the Vampire Lord, "You should realize the benefits of an alliance. Right now, Daemon doesn't know anything about what the modern Vampire World is like. You can be a bridge for him. And I'm betting that if Daemon allies with House Ravenscroft that you won't be considered exiles for much longer."

"*We*, Christian, you're a Member of House Ravenscroft, too," Balthazar reminded him. "But you're assuming that after he wakes that he won't seek out better allies."

"He might seek out *additional* allies, but he won't abandon us," Christian said with certainty.

"Because of Julian?" Arcius guessed.

"I don't know if you two realized it, but Daemon *listened* to Julian and did what Julian asked. Daemon didn't just stop from killing you on his own. He did what Julian requested of him," Christian reminded them. "Julian won't want to be parted from me. And since, as you said, I am a part of House Ravenscroft–"

"He'll stick with us, too." Balthazar tapped his chin and looked thoughtful.

"Exactly. I know you thought that Daemon would simply take Julian away, but just a few minutes with those two, tells me that Julian has far more power than Daemon in that relationship." Christian couldn't help grinning at the thought.

He wasn't surprised by this fact. Julian often played white knight and protector to his partners. Not that there had been really any serious ones. Julian had simply always been the one in charge. While Daemon might be a king and used to commanding all the Vampires, Julian would never simply follow his directions unless he agreed with them. His best friend was fiercely independent.

Arcius squeezed his large hands together. "Then everything we do to keep Daemon safe and comfortable will enhance that friendship between our House and our king."

Balthazar grunted. "Maybe so. I admit it was a surprise to see Julian stepping between Daemon and me. The boy had no fear."

"Julian is brave. Utterly brave down to his bones," Christian assured them.

Balthazar let a large, devilish grin cross his features. "Then we need to see to the king's comfort. Come, Christian, let me show you the guest house."

Balthazar took Christian down a parquet-floored hallway. It was broad and gracious with a high ceiling. There were oil portraits on the walls. Some were still lifes of fruit or flowers. Others were landscapes of waving wheat fields or ponds with a profusion of flowers peeking up from the water's surface. There were also portraits expertly done of people long dead who stared out at Christian through intelligent eyes. He wondered if any of them were Balthazar's ancestors or perhaps family to others in his House.

Speaking of others, he'd met only Ridley, Arcius and Maddie of House Ravenscroft. Elena had just been a still figure on a bed. But now as they passed by gracious rooms, he saw other Vampires inside.

There was a young man, really no more than a boy, with hair so pale it was almost white. He was laughing and talking amiably to a man that looked to be in his sixties, grizzled and dried out like a piece of old leather left in the sun too long. Both of them were sipping something red out of high ball glasses. Christian's nose found the coppery smell of blood and he knew what the liquid was. These two stopped talking and turned their heads to look at him and Balthazar pass. They stared at him with open curiosity. The boy lifted his glass to Christian. Christian nodded his head, but then quickly looked away.

Balthazar gently bumped his shoulder. "You are an object of fascination and deep curiosity. We haven't made many fledglings since being exiled. And, of course, they knew who you were before I turned you."

"How would they know me?" Christian blinked in confusion.

"Your show. They've watched your show."

Christian hadn't considered that real Vampires would be watching them. He wondered now how many of the views they got were from the lords and ladies of the night. It was a disturbing thought.

"Did they know you wanted to turn Julian and me?" he asked.

"I never publicized it, but I imagine some knew," Balthazar admitted with a shrug.

"You say that so *casually*. But you're talking about the end of Julian and my lives." Christian crossed his arms over his chest.

"End of your *First* Lives, but, trust me, though it does not seem it yet, your *Second* Life is much better."

Christian cast a glance at the Vampire Lord and saw that he actually meant what he said.

"Well, I admit, that it is rather fascinating."

Just then they passed another salon. Inside was a single tall, slender woman with black hair piled atop her patrician head. She wore a black dress and a simple choker of pearls around her swanlike throat. She, too, stared openly at him out of those strange silver eyes, but then inclined her head graciously when Balthazar greeted her.

"Who is she?" Christian asked, once they had passed by the door.

"That is Isabel. She once owned a great salon in Paris. She was dying of consumption when Oscar offered her the gift of eternal life," Balthazar murmured.

"How old is she then? And is Oscar here, too?" Christian asked.

"She's 263 years old, and, yes, Oscar is still with us. Just as a FYI, you never ask how old a Vampire is," Balthazar cautioned him.

"Why not? I understand why humans have an issue with age, but Vampires? You don't grow any older so how can it bother you?" Christian frowned at what he thought some odd carry over from human life.

"You've actually got it *reversed*. For a Vampire, the *older* you are, the *better* you are," Balthazar explained. "As we age, we get stronger. Our powers increase."

Thinking back on Balthazar's power to control a whole room of Vampires and the fact that he was head of his own House, Christian guessed he must be very old. "How old are you?"

The Vampire Lord gave him a narrow-eyed look before breaking into laughter. "Did I not just tell you that asking for a Vampire's age is a no-no?"

"Yeah, but you're very powerful and the boss here so you have to be ancient," Christian guessed.

Balthazar looked unutterably pleased. "You would think, but no. I'm an early bloomer."

Christian's brow furrowed. "Why is that?"

Balthazar shrugged. "No one knows. There are rumors out there that I'm Eyros reborn. I think that's nonsense, but I do encourage them as they keep other Vampires wary of me and my people."

"Who is Eyros?" Christian asked.

Balthazar opened his mouth in surprise, but then nodded as he must have realized that Christian knew little to nothing. "Eyros is the Immortal who founded our Bloodline. He was similar to Daemon, but could create fledglings, obviously. And, in case you're wondering, he, too, is dead. Obviously, if I am him reborn. Can't be in two places at once. Our unique gift is that of mind reading, mine control and other things like telepathy, etcetera."

"Mind control. Fascinating," Christian said and meant it. "When will I be able to use that gift?"

"It will develop with time. I would assume you will get the basic ability to lure humans to you, for instance, after you've fed from me a few times," Balthazar told him.

Balthazar proceeded to tell him about the Eleven Bloodlines, the Houses, and the relationship of Ever Dark to Earth in global terms. They had reached a pair of French doors that led outside by the time he'd explained that it was believed that time simply stopped in Ever Dark. It was never light there. The moons didn't move and electronics were faulty at the best of times. But there was technology in the Ever Dark that was so far beyond what they had on Earth that they simply considered it magic.

Christian was pleased that Balthazar didn't try to tell him that it *was* real magic, just technology that, though they could use it, they didn't really understand fully though some of the oldest Vampires had made some breakthroughs.

"Do you have any of it? Can I see some of it? Study it?" Christian had asked.

"We do not bring it here, and, unfortunately, as an exiled House, we have no access to the Ever Dark any longer," Balthazar explained.

"Well, we will now. With Daemon," Christian said, more thinking out loud than meaning to say it.

"You are very certain Daemon will be so generous with us." Balthazar's eyebrows were practically up in his hairline.

"You don't know how persuasive Julian can be. And stubborn. Very stubborn." Christian shrugged.

Balthazar grinned. "Well, I am happy to have him working on our behalf then."

Christian was tempted to say that this was perhaps better than if Julian had joined House Ravenscroft himself. But that would have poked at a still fresh wound for Balthazar. And he wasn't sure how he felt about it himself. He didn't want anything to separate him and Julian. He was certain that neither of them would allow this to. But it just made more obstacles for them.

Balthazar led him down a few steps to a gray stone path that meandered through flower beds to a large house in its own right about one hundred feet away. The large blooms bobbed in the night air. Their scent was intoxicating.

Christian forgot to ask more questions as he bent down to sniff one of the large flowers. He stared at it in the darkness. His vision was incredibly keen. He could see even its pollen. But the color was not the same as it would have been under bright sunlight. Christian felt a stab of pain.

"Christian, what is it?" One of Balthazar's hands was on his shoulders. It was a light touch, barely there, not meant to upset him, but to comfort.

"I just realized that I'll never see the sun again."

It was a stark statement. It held such grief in it. He'd just now realized one thing he had *lost*. And there was more behind it. Like an avalanche of parts of life that were now gone from him and he hadn't realized until this moment.

Balthazar drew in a breath. "No, you will not. It is the price we pay for the other things we gain by becoming lords of the night."

One of those avalanche pieces unfolded before him. His parents' faces flashed before his mind's eye.

"How do I explain this to my parents?" he asked.

His parents were brilliant professors. They were quiet, studious people with incisive minds. They *would* figure out that something was wrong with him. They would, in their way, interrogate him until he broke down. He didn't lie to them. It was simply not something he did.

How do I tell them about this?

There was a pause before Balthazar spoke, low and quiet, his hand still a surprising comforting presence on Christian's shoulder, "Normally, we break from our families."

Christian stiffened. That was not happening.

"But not always," Balthazar continued. "Some families, when they learn about the existence of Vampires, choose to join us as Acolytes. Those are our human helpers. They're our link to the day. Some of those become Vampires in the end. Others live out normal lives and have normal deaths."

He tried to imagine his scholarly parents as Vampires and couldn't do it. He assumed that not everyone was made into Vampires who wanted to be. They were chosen. Could he turn his own parents if they wanted to be chosen? His head spun with it. He clamped down on his thoughts. Thinking of his family wasn't grounding him. He would have to parse all his feelings out later.

"What about the show? The business that Julian and I have. Will we still be allowed to do that?" Christian asked.

"Of course. You can even still, well, *pretend* to look for Vampires," Balthazar let out a slightly breathy laugh. "People look younger for longer now. No one will question your youthful looks for at least a decade, if not longer. We'll have to, eventually, arrange for you to phase out of that part of your lives."

"Right, of course, makes sense." Christian stood up. He dusted his hands on the fronts of his pants. "There's a lot to think about."

"There is," Balthazar agreed. "But you have *time*, Christian. It'll all work out."

The Vampire Lord then reached out and brushed his fingers across the tip of Christian's nose. Christian frowned.

"I thought we were going to take the touching thing slow," he said.

Balthazar smirked. "You had pollen on your nose, but I won't save you from silliness again–"

"Thanks for doing that. Pollen removal is allowable at any time."

Christian scrubbed his nose with his right hand. The truth was that he was missing Balthazar's hand on his shoulder and was cursing himself for it.

"Good to know."

They resumed walking again to the guest house. There were lights on in every window though the shades were drawn and all Christian could see were occasional silhouettes.

"Some of our human Acolytes live on the premises for a time and offer to feed us," Balthazar explained as he gestured towards the house. "We often don't allow any one of them to stay more than three months."

Christian frowned. He was relieved that the Vampires weren't *killing* them. "Why not?"

"Being fed from can become quite addictive especially from an Eyros."

"Why do I have a feeling that every Bloodline says that?"

Balthazar flashed him a smile, his white teeth practically glowing in the moonlight. "But *we* are actually right."

"Because of the mind control thing?"

"I would touch your nose again as I said, bingo, but there's no pollen there any longer. And yes, you are correct. Not only is the feeding physically pleasurable, but we also implant thoughts to make it more so."

"But that's–"

"Mind control, yes, Christian, it's what we do. As a proud member of the Eyros Bloodline, you will learn to do it, too." Balthazar flashed him another unapologetic grin. "It doesn't hurt them. Just makes things better."

"Do you tell them you're doing it?"

"Sometimes. Most know." Balthazar shrugged.

"I don't know how I feel about that. It's one thing if the person consents to it, but another if they don't." Christian hunched their shoulders.

"I assure you that every person wishes to be here of their own free will," Balthazar told him.

They were at the front door now. It was painted a deep brick red and had a highly polished brass knocker and handle. Balthazar didn't use the handle. Instead, he simply opened the door and pushed it inwards, gesturing for Christian to precede him.

Christian stepped inside to a large foyer. Flowers, likely from the garden, filled delicate oriental style vases and gave the room a sweet scent. The walls that were painted a deep royal blue. The floor was marble with an inset design of a compass. There were more oil paintings here with dark frames showing nautical scenes. The light came from a chandelier that was set on low and large pillar candles on various tables. It gave the place a pleasant, mellow appeal. Christian actually found himself relaxing.

That was until he saw a woman, dressed in flowing white pants and a white wrap shirt, coming towards them out of a hallway that stretched deeper into the house. She had honey-blond hair that hung loose to her shoulders, a mouth that was slightly too wide to make her classically pretty, a smattering of freckles over a pert nose and two bright green eyes.

Even if he hadn't seen the green eyes, Christian would have known she was human and not a Vampire. Every Vampire–including himself he imagined now–moved in a certain graceful, almost liquid-boned way that humans simply couldn't replicate. Her face was slightly familiar to him. It didn't click that he knew her until she spoke.

"Welcome, Masters," she intoned. Her voice was smooth and low, but then she saw Christian and she gaped at him for a half a moment before sputtering out, "Christian?! Christian, is that you? It's me! Laura! Laura Shelty. We went to highschool together and I've watched your show with Julian forever. What are you doing here? Are you an Acolyte as well?" But then she really *looked* at him and one of her hands fluttered up to her mouth. "You're–you're a member of House Ravenscroft?! Oh, my God!"

She quickly dropped down to her knees, forehead brushing the floor. Christian stared at her now in open-mouthed shock.

In that sudden silence, Balthazar murmured, "And *this* is why we usually don't turn people in the same city as they were living before. Awkward moments."

Seeing Laura on her knees, Christian had to agree with him. How many more of these "awkward moments" would there be? He was betting a lot more.

SIREN SONG

*J*ulian allowed his fingertips to drift over the back of Daemon's right hand. The skin was soft. His fingers slid back to a wrist that was surprisingly fine-boned, but strong. Despite this, he couldn't encircle it with his fingers. Daemon was large all over.

Julian shifted his gaze to Daemon's face for the five-hundredth time and studied what he saw there. The Vampire King's eyelids were still closed. His dark, long lashes fanned against high cheekbones. Daemon's skin had a slightly golden cast though sunlight had never touched it as far as Julian knew. Aversion to sunlight seemed to be one of the myths that were true about Vampires. But maybe the Vampire King could withstand sunlight, too, another difference between Vampires and Immortals. Or maybe to look sun-burnished was just another gift the Vampire King had.

Daemon's jaw was strongly defined, tapering to a well-made chin. His lips were sinfully sensual and a soft rose color that made Julian think they might taste sweet. His nose was noble, straight and long. He had a broad, clear forehead that indicated intelligence, but also passion. Julian remembered again how Daemon had come into this world–this room, actually–smashing through the wall between worlds in the guise of an army of wolves only to simply overwhelm a powerful Vampire like Lord Balthazar Ravenscroft with utter ease. Those were the actions of a passionate man.

But is it because he cares so deeply about me or did he simply not want something that he considers his to be taken away?

Julian believed it was likely the latter. Daemon didn't know him well enough to care for him. Julian wasn't upset by this fact. Even though he was far more romantic–at least on the *outside*–than Christian, he wasn't a fool.

And yet...

I came for you.

Julian shivered at those remembered words of Daemon's. They held such power. Such simple words. Yet they meant so much. Julian shut his eyelids and shook his head.

What am I doing? I do not know him. I hated Vampires just yesterday. And here I am wondering if one of them might care for me! Half hoping he does!

With Julian's eyes closed, his other senses increased and he could smell his spit up from earlier on the shirt he wore. His nose wrinkled and he looked down at the ruined clothing. He plucked at them with distaste.

I need a shower and a new set of clothes.

Christian had already put on the bed some drawstring pants and a long sleeved shirt that would likely fit him. Balthazar was about his same size. He knew where the bathroom was from seeing where Balthazar had gone to get him water. But his nose would have led him there in any case. He realized he could smell shampoo and soap quite clearly emanating from the dark doorway opposite the bed.

Julian studied Daemon's face one last time, wondering if it was safe to leave him, if only for a quick shower. He was still unconscious. There was no change from earlier that he could see.

He'll be fine, he told himself. *He wouldn't have risked his life just to stop me from drinking from Balthazar. That would be insane. He's just tired. Right. Tired.*

The bag of blood was still halfway full and was dripping into the Vampire Lord's arm so that wouldn't need to be changed anytime soon. Maddie had left them to check on Elena again. He thought of calling her back while he cleaned up. Hopefully, she could watch Daemon while he bathed. He really couldn't bear to stink of blood any longer. He stood up.

And found a hand gripping his right wrist.

His head snapped towards Daemon's face. The Vampire King's glowing red eyes were fixed upon him.

"You're awake!" Julian cried unnecessarily, but he was thrilled it was true. Daemon was awake! He really wasn't dying or hurting too badly. At least, that clear, intent gaze didn't show any pain or sickness or weakness at all. "Let me call Maddie and–"

Where were you going?

It took Julian a second to register that Daemon's lips were not moving and to decipher the meaning of the words. Daemon hadn't opened his mouth once.

"Why don't you speak out loud?" Julian asked.

One of those elegant, expressive eyebrows rose. *It is more efficient speaking mind to mind. Is it not?*

"Not really. No one else seems to be able to hear you except me," Julian pointed out.

You are the only one I care to speak to within this den of thieves, Daemon answered, his eyes hooding. *Now where were you going, fledgling?*

It was Julian's turn to raise an eyebrow. He let out a startled laugh as he repeated, "Den of thieves? I assume you are saying that, because Balthazar was going to feed me. But remember–"

That hand tightened on his wrist. *Let us never speak of that again. You will never feed from another Master. You will never–*

"Now hold on!" Julian's temper flared. "I can feed from whoever I want! And considering you're still too weak to feed me now, I'm going to have to feed from someone else so–"

Daemon was suddenly sitting up. The bag of blood had levitated from the stand and was in hand. That mouth that had not opened to

19

speak opened to tear the top of the bag off with ease. White fangs flashed as he drank down the entire bag in one gulp.

The cooler near the side of the bed that contained more blood packs was suddenly flying to Daemon's hands, too. The lid flipped open and Daemon did the same to the half dozen bags inside as he'd done to the first. His eyes, which had been the color of banked coals before, were glowing like living flames as he finished the last.

Julian blinked rapidly. "Did you just... I suppose after the wolf thing that I *shouldn't* be surprised that you can move things with your mind, too, but– but fucking *hell*! It's like you used the Force or–"

Daemon's hand was under his chin, cutting off his flow of words. It was not a violent touch. It was incredibly gentle. The touch told Julian that he was *treasured*. He met those burning eyes.

You will only feed from me, Daemon's mind voice was quiet.

"If you're strong enough," Julian answered just as quietly, but with as much force. "I'm not putting you in danger again. You can't make me do that. Are we clear?"

Daemon finally inclined his head, breaking the stare down that had, unconsciously, been occurring between them and he released Julian's chin. The loss of that touch felt strange. Almost as if something was missing.

Agreed, the Vampire King said.

"You–you agree? Just like that?" Julian had expected a fight.

I respect your desire to protect me. Not that it is necessary, the Vampire King said. *We need to get more blood.* He made a face as he looked at the scattered bags on the bed. *From a person. Not these contrivances.*

"Yeah, I thought they were pretty gross, too," Julian agreed.

I am sure you did find them quite unappetizing. You are too young to be drinking from anyone but me... even if I was inclined to allow it, Daemon explained.

Julian shook his head as another flare of irritation lit up in his chest like a match being struck. "Just when I think we're starting to understand one another, you're making proclamations again!"

You are my fledgling. I am both your Master and your king. Making proclamations is what I do. Daemon's plush lips were curled into a surprisingly endearing smile.

The irritation died away as quickly as it had sprung up and Julian found himself smiling back. "Well, just so you're aware that what I do is go my own way. I'll follow yours if it makes sense. But nobody rules me. I bow to no king. You will have to earn my respect, just like anyone else. In fact, it will be far harder for you, because you're actually demanding fealty."

I will take that as a challenge, Daemon answered, still smiling and appearing more pleased. *It is good that you have fire in you. My fledgling should be strong in both mind and body, intelligent and beautiful.*

Julian found himself coloring, caught completely off guard by the compliment. "Ah,well, compared to you, I look like leftovers, but okay."

Daemon looked at Julian through those dark, long lashes. *I look forward to showing you just how beautiful I find you.*

Julian was stunned at the comment once more. Heat though flared in between his legs. Daemon was probably the most beautiful person he'd ever met, but he also had a strength and power that Julian hadn't been exposed to before. He was used to being the one stronger than his partner. The thought of being pursued by someone who topped him in all ways–or, at least, wanted to–was a surprising thrill.

Before Julian could respond to the blatant flirting, the Vampire King was speaking again, *But first, you were thinking of going somewhere when you thought I was sleeping. It must have been important for you to leave as you have been a very keen watcher.*

"I wanted to make sure you were okay," Julian admitted. That act had his shirt ruffling and the scent of vomit rising up from the material. His nose wrinkled again. "But I stink to high heaven. I want to shower and change."

He gestured to the clothes on the bed. Daemon picked up the shirt and *sniffed* it. A frown crossed his handsome features.

"What's wrong?"

It smells like him. Daemon was holding the offending garment with two fingers as if it stunk.

"You mean that it smells like Balthazar? Well, yeah, those are his clothes. Mine are back at my house," he answered and reached for the "offending garment".

Daemon kept it just out of his reach, still frowning. *I do not like for you to smell of him.*

"Yeah, well, he and I are the same size and I don't want to smell like vomit any longer. So you're going to have to deal." Julian yanked the shirt from Daemon's hand and grabbed the pants before the Vampire King decided that those offended him, too.

He will think you are showing him favor by wearing his things. Daemon was still frowning.

"Balthazar can think what he likes, though I'm *not* showing him favor by borrowing a shirt and pants. I'm grateful he turned Christian and for his help in general. Did you see what he did in the Siryn Blood Den? He didn't have to come get me, but he did," Julian reminded him.

He wished you for himself. A pair of beauties. Do not think he acted out of charity. Daemon waved away Balthazar's actions as if they were nothing. Julian found that unfair.

"You probably are right on one level. But I think you're judging him a lot more harshly than you would have if he hadn't been trying to feed me–per *my* request–remember?" Julian said.

I am his king. The other–the big one–understood that immediately. Balthazar had no thought of the offense he would be giving me by his wrongful actions. The Vampire King's eyes blazed.

"Arcius is a priest though. He's big into faith, I think. Balthazar didn't believe you even existed," Julian said. "He just thought you were some old Vampire that abandoned me. He really didn't–maybe even doesn't–think you're the Daemon in all the stories."

The Vampire King slid his legs off of the bed and appeared to be contemplating standing. Julian felt a twinge of worry that he would not be strong enough. But then Daemon got up gracefully without a quiver.

What do you mean that he does not believe I exist?

Julian had to look up to see Daemon's face. His nose only came to

Daemon's shoulder. It was a little unnerving how *big* the Vampire King was. But his physical prowess seemed to be nothing compared to the things he could do without moving a muscle.

Julian scrubbed the back of his head as he realized the minefield he'd likely just walked into. Sophia had told him the tragic history of the Immortals and the Vampires in a dispassionate way, and, while parts had been terrible to hear, they weren't *personal* to him. The other ten Immortals hadn't been his friends and confidants. They hadn't been the people he had relied upon to feed him.

Again, one of those hands was beneath his chin. A connection–or rather, a greater connection–when their skin touched was created. Julian felt a *zing* of electricity go through him that seemed to short circuit his thoughts.

You do not wish to tell me something. Daemon studied his face minutely.

"No, I don't, because I have some bad news," Julian answered truthfully with a sigh. "I'm not even sure how to begin."

The other Immortals... I do not sense them. Their cities are on lockdown, Daemon muttered as if to himself more than to Julian. *And they had not come to Nightvallen for some time. They would not abandon me unless they were unable to come to my side. What have you heard of their fate?*

"There was an uprising," Julian explained. "Some, or maybe even all of the Immortals, were... killed."

He then repeated all he had heard from Sophia Strange. After he was done, long moments ticked by while Daemon stared down at him, unblinking. Julian had no idea what he was thinking. Perhaps he had made a mistake telling him all of this when he was still weak. But then Daemon was moving again, like normal.

No. Immortals do not die, Daemon denied. *Not like you are thinking. But perhaps their coils were slain...*

"Are they reincarnated? Balthazar is said to be Eyros reborn," Julian remarked and immediately regretted it. Complimenting the Vampire Lord seemed to raise Daemon's ire. "Not that I think this, but–"

He thinks this? Daemon grunted in mirthless amusement. *He dreams of it, I am sure.*

"He's pretty powerful. Not as powerful as you, but he was able to save everybody here from a crazy Master and has survived in exile, so he's got something going on for sure," Julian pointed out, not sure why he was defending Balthazar so much. Maybe it was because he was Christian's Master and that meant Daemon and him *needed* to get along.

He killed his Master? Daemon's eyebrows rose.

"It was warranted. The guy was hurting everyone in his House. Beating them. Starving them. I'm certain that Balthazar is telling the truth about that. Considering that others came with him into exile instead of staying in the Ever Dark sounds like he can generate some loyalty."

Daemon's brow clouded. *He must be... No, his Master must have simply been weak. I do not believe...*

But the Vampire King looked thoughtful and not so inclined to judge Balthazar badly at that moment anyways.

I just hope that Balthazar doesn't speak a lot near him, Julian thought. *That might wipe away all the good I just did.*

"Hey, I'm going to quickly shower and then we can get you more blood. If you want to lay down again for a moment–"

Before Julian could finish his sentence, Daemon was striding towards the bathroom door. *There is a bathing area here?*

"Uhm, yeah." Julian had to practically jog to keep up with him. "Let me turn on the lights."

No need. There are candles.

"Yeah, but–"

The candles suddenly burst into flame. They were placed strategically around the bathroom and gave off plenty of light to cast the large room in a golden glow. Julian wasn't surprised to see that the room was plush. Balthazar seemed like the kind of person to have the best of everything. He also seemed as if he enjoyed being incredibly clean.

There was a walk-in shower with rain showerhead, but also jets on every wall but the one made of glass. There was also a huge claw-footed tub. There was a vast vanity, lined with colognes and lotions, with a sea-shell shaped sink set into the very porcelain. Julian set the shirt and pants there. There was also a toilet and separate bidet.

So Vampires do go to the bathroom. Wow. Okay. Didn't expect that. Or maybe this is for his human guests.

Daemon was staring at the toilet and bidet with interest. Julian stepped over to him.

"Those are used for... ah, well, when you go to the bathroom." Realizing that likely meant *nothing* to Daemon as it was a euphemism, he explained haltingly, "Humans, uhm, you know that they excrete waste and... Well, these are to remove the waste from the home to the sewer system. This one here." He gestured to the bidet. "Helps to, ah, clean their, uhm, excreting parts."

Yes, this is a similar system to what we have.

"Really? There are toilets in Nightvallen?"

Daemon did not answer. Instead he pushed the metal handle for the toilet and watched the water swirl down the bottom. He did it again. And again. And again. Julian was reminded of a cat as Daemon's eyes flickered along with the water.

"It flushes it into the sewers, see?" Julian dropped a piece of toilet paper into the water and both of them watched as it swirled away.

Daemon grabbed one of the cut glass bottles of cologne and was about to drop that into the toilet when Julian quickly took it from him.

"Don't do that! It would get stuck and water would overflow. It just wouldn't be good," he finished when Daemon continued to look at him without blinking.

Do you suppose losing that cologne would displease Balthazar? There was a curious little glint in Daemon's eye that made Julian nervous.

"It *would* and that's why we're *not* going to mess with his stuff," Julian replied firmly. He set the bottle back where Daemon had taken it from.

Daemon shrugged as if it didn't matter. He then shocked Julian by pulling off the tank cover of the toilet.

"Whoa! What are you doing now?"

Julian tried to get him to put it down, but that was unsuccessful. Daemon flushed the toilet again and watched as the water in the tank drained into the bowl. The Vampire King grunted and replaced the tank cover, satisfied that he understood how it worked, at least in part. He then pressed the button on the bidet that sent a stream of water shooting up into the air.

One would sit on this, I take it.

"Yep."

Quite ingenious.

"If you think bathrooms are cool, I can't wait to show you computers and all the rest."

Julian suddenly realized that Daemon had a *mountain* of things to learn. From modern plumbing to cars to planes to the internet How would the Vampire King react to a world that was nothing like the one he'd left? His curiosity was a good thing. It indicated an elasticity of mind. He also wasn't afraid of anything. In fact, Daemon was now over by the sink.

Daemon turned the handles and watched as hot and cold water sprayed into the sea-shell shaped sink. Before Julian had a chance to even move, the Vampire King was checking out the glass enclosed shower. The bathtub had barely warranted a glance, probably because he recognized what it was. He was opening the shower door, stepping inside and reaching for the faucet handles again before Julian *saved* him from being sprayed in the face.

"Hey! Do you want to get wet? The water will come out of there, there and there." He pointed to the nozzles. Daemon stepped out of the shower and watched as Julian adjusted all the knobs and water spurted out everywhere. He got the sleeve of his shirt wet but it didn't matter, because he was already going to change out of this one anyways. He tested the water with his fingers and adjusted it until it was the right temperature. At least what he liked anyways. "How about if I shower first and then if you'd like to try it you can–"

Why do we not bathe together?

Julian heard the slither of the long fur coat Daemon wore leaving his broad shoulders and sliding to the floor. That was followed by the slap of leather on marble as the Vampire King shimmied out of the rest of his clothes. All of this happened, before Julian even had the chance to turn around. When he did turn, he found the Vampire King was stripped completely. Julian's mouth went dry. Daemon's body was even more magnificent than Julian had remembered.

Long, muscular legs. An eight-pack–not *six* but *eight* defined valleys and hills–stomach. Firm, broad pecs. Magnificent arms. And of course, the thing that had Julian staring in utmost amazement before he could catch himself was the long, thick cock that hung between Daemon's legs. That cock stirred awake as he watched, plumping and reddening as blood engorged it.

Undress, Daemon murmured. *Or would you like me to do so for you?*

Julian again seemed unable to keep up with the Vampire King. Daemon's fingers were underneath the hem of his shirt and he was raising it above Julian's head with a rush of air. His pants and under-wear were similarly gone before he noticed. Daemon hadn't even had the shoes and socks to slow him down as Christian had eased those off of Julian earlier when he'd collapsed. Now he and the Vampire King were standing, naked, and inches apart.

Daemon's fingers were at Julian's temples. They slowly slid down Julian's cheeks and then under his chin. The Vampire King's eyes were glowing in the near darkness of the bathroom.

I have waited for you for millennia, he whispered. *All this time. And, finally, you are here. I almost lost you.*

That whisper seemed to caress Julian's mind. He almost closed his eyes as the words wrapped around every neuron.

"So you're sure that I'm going to live? Certain you can invest in me now?" Julian asked, bitterness breaking through. He felt a stab of pain from the Vampire King and, immediately, cursed himself. "I'm sorry. I shouldn't have said that–"

You are angry with me? It was more a statement than a question. *Because I left you for a time?*

"You owed me nothing more than what you gave," Julian answered.

But you still are wounded, because I held back when you needed me to be

27

fully there. I understand. Daemon's head lowered and he was silent. Finally, he spoke again, *I will do everything I can to heal this rift between us if you let me.*

Those fingers on his skin were causing electric sparks to course through Julian's body, making it hard to think, hard to control what he felt and said and did.

"It scares me how *intense* this thing is between us sometimes. I feel like I'm falling," Julian admitted, the words flowing out so easily. "I don't know you yet. So this can't be... be natural."

Daemon's mouth–that plush, gorgeous mouth–curled into a smile. *It is perfectly natural between fledgling and Master.*

"I don't want to be doing something because I'm being–being *compelled* to do it!" Julian crossed his arms over his chest, but somehow it made him feel more vulnerable rather than less.

To his surprise, Daemon nodded in understanding. *Nor would I. That is not what this is. Could I compel you? Yes. Could I make you love me? Yes. And I could make it so you'd never realize I had done any of it. You would think you were acting of your own free will.*

A chill went through Julian. He thought of the ease with which Daemon killed those two Vampires. His ability to become an army of wolves. The way he had held up Balthazar like the Vampire Lord had weighed–and was as frightening–as a newly born kitten. Not to mention the ability to levitate objects and cause candles to burn on their own. What else could Daemon do?

"I should be frightened of you, shouldn't I?" Julian asked.

The fingers underneath his chin became a hand cupping his cheek. *Never. You are my treasure. My one. My fledgling. I will keep you safe above all things. What you feel towards me is our connection. Not compulsion. Our fate to be with one another throughout all eternity.*

And, for a moment, Julian could see that future together. The adventures in Ever Dark and on Earth. He and Daemon would explore every inch of those worlds and maybe more. They would know them like the backs of their hands. No mystery would be too great for them. They would have endless oceans of time to discover everything.

We are destined, Julian Harrow, to be together.

Daemon's left hand was now cupping his other cheek. The Vampire King leaned down. He did so slowly, giving Julian every chance to get away. Julian stayed where he was. No compulsion. No unnatural need. This beautiful, dangerous creature wanted him... and Julian wanted him back. The Vampire King was the ultimate adventure and Julian would not back away from him.

I want to step into your darkness, Julian found himself saying.

I will set worlds on fire to lead you to me, Daemon answered.

The kiss, when it came, made Julian *shake*.

Julian could feel Daemon's fangs rasping against his tongue. They were sharp and alien and yet so right. His own fangs suddenly came out, his jaw aching with the need to *bite*. The thought of blood, which had been so horrifying before, had saliva filling his mouth now.

He imagined the *meatiness* of Daemon's blood, the hot gush of it as it broke free of the prison of the Vampire King's body and raced down his throat, and the tingling sensation as it was absorbed and became a part of him. His heart pounded like a drum. He swore that the whole house must be able to hear it. The sound was transmitted to his cock and it rose between them of its own accord.

Julian's hands were suddenly gripping the Vampire King's shoulders. He pulled Daemon into the shower. Hot water gushed over them. It massaged their sides and backs like an expert masseuse. Everything seemed to be liquid heat.

Julian's mouth left Daemon's and he was biting down the column of the Vampire King's throat. He lingered at the hollow, lapping at the water that collected there in crystal clear droplets. He placed the points of his fangs against that soft as silk skin. Daemon hissed. The Vampire King's head was tilted back, offering himself to Julian. The beat of his pulse radiated upwards through Julian's fangs. It mixed with his own heartbeat until it felt like there was no difference between them.

All he had to do was gently bite down and the blood–the blood of the king–would flow into his mouth and down his throat. It would pool in his belly like hot port wine and he would grow drunk with it. The siren call to feed swam through his veins and arteries.

"NO!"

Julian wrenched himself away so that his cheek was pressed against the cold marble tile. His fingers gripped the stone as he kept his back to Daemon. The Vampire King's heat was suddenly against him again.

"No," Julian growled.

What is it, my one?

"I promised I wouldn't feed from you until you're fed, remember?" Julian's voice was ragged, barely recognizable to himself with all the need in it.

Daemon's hands ran up and down his spine. *I remember. But you are in need and I would give you–*

"I know! And that's why I must say no." Julian let out a hoarse laugh. "All that power you have, Vampire King, and yet, here I am, a little *nothing*, with all this power over *you*."

Daemon chuckled. His mouth was at the top of Julian's spine. His breath felt hotter than the water. *You have discovered the trick, Julian. I am yours as much as you are mine.*

"I have pledged never to hurt you like you have never to hurt me," Julian got out even as his fangs *ached* and his belly *burned*. "So don't tempt me. Please help me keep my promise to you."

All right. Then let us get you clean and go on the hunt. Daemon's one hand stroked his hair. *I will provide for you, my own, my one. You will see. You will feel. You will know.*

30

FIRST KISS

"Laura, please rise. You're making my fledgling very uncomfortable," Balthazar murmured as he urged the Acolyte to her feet.

Christian had gone still in that way of his that indicated that he wanted to physically take himself out of the equation. Balthazar was in the very early stages of learning his fledgling's true personality, but one thing that was becoming very clear to Balthazar wasn't that Christian felt little, but instead felt too *much*. Christian resorted to logic, because his emotions were simply too much for him. It was a way to distance himself from what was happening. When people or things were out of place, Christian *felt* that on a deep empathic level. Like Laura being here and bowing. That was unnerving his very intelligent, emotional fledgling and he would put a stop to it.

She jumped up with alacrity, which didn't surprise Balthazar. She was always eager to please him most of all. Seeing Christian had thrown her, too. "Oh! I'm sorry! So sorry! I just–I just–didn't mean to address him so informally and–and–"

"It's okay, Laura. I'm glad you did," Christian said stiffly, but he tried smiling along with it, which Balthazar almost found painful in and of itself. "There's no need to call me 'Master' or whatever. That would be... weird. Christian is fine. We were schoolmates after all."

Laura was biting her lower lip through Christian's attempts to put her at ease and on the same level. Christian didn't understand but the formalities were important to the Acolytes. Breeding too much familiarity caused *hopes* to rise. Balthazar had found that out himself. In fact, he had relearned that lesson not all that long ago.

"Quite, if that's what you wish, Ma–Christian," she said awkwardly. She cast about a little and then remembered how she was to behave with them. "Are you here to feed, company or both? I know that Rey is missing you very much, Master Balthazar."

Balthazar grimaced before he smoothed his face into one of blandness again. Rey was one of those misplaced hopes. He was certain that all of the Acolytes had already heard that he had taken a fledgling, Rey, above all, would be aware of it. Rey had hopes that *he* would be taken. Balthazar had toyed with the idea at the beginning, now that he had Christian, he couldn't imagine bringing in Rey.

While Laura did not catch his reaction, his very clever fledgling did. Christian raised an eyebrow. He gave a brief shake of his head, an indication that they would discuss it later.

Or not at all. That would be best. Not at all. I will have to deal with Rey. He cannot stay here. It may be best if he is relieved of his memories of this place and me altogether.

"No, Laura, I think I'd like Sheila to come join us in the Deep Suite," he answered smoothly, even as his mind went to unhappy places.

He liked Rey, but an unhappy Acolyte could poison others with unhappiness. It was best that it did not happen. Unlike Rey, Sheila was steady and had no desire to become a Vampire. She would be a non-sexual, comforting presence in the room with him and Christian.

Laura did a little curtsey. "I'll send up water and wine. Anything else?"

He shook his head. "And don't worry about taking us there. I'll show Christian the way."

Laura did another little curtsey, quickly turned on her heels and headed into the house. Balthazar put a guiding hand on Christian's lower back. He felt the muscles beneath his palm go tense, but then quickly relaxed. While he would respect Christian's need for boundaries, they had to be able to touch one another.

"What are we doing? I thought we were getting humans set up for Daemon to feed from."

There was a very cute frown on Christian's lips. Balthazar knew he should not find that frown *cute*. Christian would not like it. But it was nonetheless.

"We will. But first, I need to feed you and it's best I feed myself first," Balthazar said as he directed Christian towards a set of sweeping mahogany stairs that led to the second floor. "And this will be a valuable lesson. You'll get to see how I feed from humans."

"Will I get to feed from Sheila, too, then?"

Balthazar shook his head and sighed. "You know very well you will not be allowed to. You feed from *me* and me alone."

"Of course. Of course, I know that. I just–"

"Want your freedom as soon as possible?" Yes, that *was* bitterness in his tone.

But Christian surprised him by shaking his head. "No, I just want to make sure I have as many options as possible in case… in case we're separated for some reason."

"We are *not* going to be separated for *any* reason." Balthazar hadn't intended his tone to be so sharp, but the very thought of Christian being taken from him was intolerable.

Yet Christian wasn't about to simply allow the subject to drop. "But Daemon is now here. We're being hunted by this Order. We don't know what could–"

"We will *not* be separated," Balthazar repeated. Christian was correct about what all could go wrong, but Balthazar refused to have any of it right now. "Worrying about such a slim possibility is not useful, Christian."

"I wasn't worried. Not in the way you're assuming. I was just considering all angles. I'm sorry I upset you. I just like to be prepared. When Julian and I go on missions we consider everything that could happen and then go a step beyond that," Christian explained.

"Doesn't it distress you even a little to think of being separated from me?" He knew he should not have asked that as soon as the words left his mouth. He sounded needy. It was quite ridiculous for him–who had been called a cad too many times to count–was now pathetically pawing at Christian's pant leg.

Christian's lips opened, shut, opened, shut again. Finally, he said, "I was going to brain Daemon with a lamp to save you."

Balthazar let out a laugh. "While appreciated, what does that have to do with anything?"

"It shows that my feelings towards you are growing in a positive direction," Christian offered.

"Ah. Lamp bashing. A sign of impending affection."

"You don't think I'm moving fast enough towards liking you? You want me to swoon over you, but I bet that you grow bored with people who do that anyways." Christian swept a hand through the air.

"I don't!" He thought of Rey. Was it true? Did he grow bored quickly? No, it was just that Rey was *not* the one, but Christian was.

"Then what was that look you got on your face when Laura mentioned this Rey person?" Christian had paused halfway up the staircase.

"Rey is another matter as is having Laura call you by your first name." Balthazar tried to get them moving again.

Christian imitated a stump. "What are you talking about?"

Balthazar glanced around to see if anyone was near then he listened for familiar heartbeats. None. "We shouldn't discuss this here. But I will say that there is a *balance* between Vampire and Acolyte. And if you break that, then expectations can be set that are very difficult to erase. Actually, it's easy to erase them, considering we're Eyros, but it causes upset."

"I don't understand. You're saying that having Laura call me Christian instead of Master is the same as whatever happened between you and Rey?" Christian's eyebrows rose to his hairline.

"I'm saying that large things start small. Come on. Upstairs.

Enough stalling. I can hear your stomach grumbling from here." Balthazar made a shooing motion toward Christian to urge him up the stairs.

"I am not stalling. What is this Deep Suite?" Christian asked, still not moving.

"That's the *last* question I will answer on the stairs. So enjoy it. The Deep Suite is the innermost suite in the back of the house," he said. "I like it best because it's a calming space."

"You like to be calm when you're having sex and feeding?" Christian's eyebrows rose.

Balthazar let out a bark of laughter. His fledgling was direct. He should remember that. "That's *another* question. But just for fun, I'll answer it. Yes, I *do*. The line between sex and violence, feeding and violence, is very thin. So I like things to be peaceful. When I was first turned, we killed the humans we fed from more often than not. The killing was part of the experience."

"Your Master... Roan Tithe, right? He made you do that, didn't he?" Christian's voice was a bare whisper, but it held a note of horror and sympathy.

"Yes, he did," his voice was flat. It often went that way when talking about Roan, even if he tried to control it. "But he was also of his time. Many of the Vampires made during the Wars were violent. That's all they knew. He was of that class."

"That doesn't excuse–"

"No, it doesn't. I killed him. I *ended* him because there are limits that I believe must be honored. Many Vampires don't feel as I do," Balthazar explained, though he knew that it was hardly an explanation at all. There was so much that Christian didn't know about Vampires. So much he might hate. But Balthazar wanted him to fall in love with the night first so that when he found the ugly parts that he'd survive the blow easier. "I have rules, Christian, that we treat the Acolytes with respect. That we don't hurt them. If we can help it. That we don't mess with their minds. Unless we must."

"Then I'm even more glad it was you who turned me," Christian breathed.

More glad. More...

For the first time, Christian touched *him*. Balthazar held very still. It was just a brief brush of fingertips along his right cheek. Brief and gone. But it happened. He resisted touching that cheek. It was a sure bet it wouldn't happen again if he did.

Christian shifted from foot to foot. "Shouldn't we go to this Deep Suite?"

Balthazar blinked. He'd gotten lost in the moment. "Yes, yes, let's do that."

They walked down a hallway to a set of double doors that led into the Deep Suite. Balthazar could sense over half a dozen Vampire denizens in the house being fed or having sex or doing some combination of both. The earthy scent of musk mixed with the coppery rich scent of blood was tantalizing and dangerous. He quickly reached over and opened the doors. Like he had when they'd entered the house, Balthazar allowed Christian to precede him.

His fledgling stepped into the suite. The walls were a cool light blue called Dream. He'd thought the paint name stupid, but whenever he rested in this suite he did have good dreams. Oddly, they were dreams of walking by the sea, holding onto someone's hand, smiling, feeling complete. He never saw the person's face. He knew it was a man. But that was all.

Balthazar came inside and closed the doors behind them as Christian stood in the middle of the center room of the suite, taking in the space. The floor was polished to a high gloss. There was a round rug with an intricate design in blues and grays. There were no windows. Glass could break. The light in the room mimicked dusk or dawn.

Directly ahead of them was a large sofa with deep cushions that would allow two people to lay down side by side. There were two overly large loveseats facing the sofa and several low coffee tables of white stone. Intricate bonsai trees dotted the room, bringing the outside in.

There were abstract paintings on the wall. A stripe of red. A slash of blue. A faded peach like the sunrise he'd just seen. To the right was the door to a vast bedroom with a four poster bed in similar colors.

To the left was a bathroom just as large as the bedroom. A shower that could fit six. It was a comfortable space.

"It is calming," Christian said as he slowly turned to face Balthazar. "Reminds me of a mixture of a high end spa and a house of ill repute."

Another bark of laughter exited his lips. "Been to many houses of ill repute, have you, Christian?"

High color appeared on Christian's cheeks, but he answered, "Not many. Okay, not any. It's what I imagine one would look like. I can smell *sex*. These enhanced senses are quite keen. And I can even hear the slap of skin and, ah, grunts."

Balthazar's lips twitched, but he tried not to smile. His little scientist was learning. "Yes, quite."

"Have you been in many houses of ill repute?" Christian looked up at him through his dark lashes. Those lashes should have been criminal. They were so effective in distracting him.

"Oh, god, yes, of course," he answered.

Christian's eyes widened. "Truly?"

"Back in my day, there was to be no sex before marriage. Not with the women you were to marry in your class. And, certainly, not with the lads that attracted me." He smoothed his hands down his front.

"But if you went to a whorehouse then you *were* having sex before marriage. But I suppose it didn't count," Christian answered his own question.

"Exactly. What you did in those places was simply not discussed if you were a young man with blue blood and enough coin to silence mouths." He shrugged. "It was a different time. Now, there's no need for it. People are open to most anything."

"How do you make Acolytes? How do you decide who is going to be one? I mean... Laura? I remember her as a nice, if nondescript girl, in high school." Christian's eyes were bright with interest. "How do you know if someone will keep your secret rather than running to the media? The Eyros can control minds, but not every Vampire can do that, right?"

"Every Vampire can control human minds to a certain extent. It's called Seduction. But yes, it is much easier for an Eyros to make an offer to a human than let's say a Kaly. Though the Kaly would likely just kill the human and reanimate their corpse."

"Reanimate–"

He waved the inevitable question away. "That's going too far afield. I told you about the powers that each Bloodline has. That's theirs. But the thing is that we can take more chances with the people we turn to our side than the others. We can wipe the minds of those who end up not working out."

Like Rey...

"But is there something that you see in that person? Clearly, you don't take in everyone," Christian pointed out.

Balthazar nodded. "You're right. We mostly pick those in power like politicians or the wealthy. We also target those professions that we need like doctors, lawyers and police officers. We also heavily influence the military. Don't want them going after us in the end. Not that most Vampires couldn't just retreat to the Ever Dark and strike out for humans when needed, but still better to nip that in the bud."

"Laura isn't any of those things. She's *normal*. Maybe even boring," Christian said with a curl of his lip.

"True. You see then there are the Acolytes we choose because their personalities indicate they would be willing to be fed from," Balthazar said and watched Christian's reaction.

A frown line appeared on Christian's forehead and he wasn't surprised. This would be difficult for someone like Christian, who restricted who touched him–or even looked at him–might not be able to put himself into these types of Acolyte's headspaces.

"They *want* to be fed from?" Christian clarified.

"They love it. They want to surrender. Or be made to surrender," he said.

Christian scrubbed his face with those elegant hands. "Is there always sex with feeding?"

"That's a very good question. Why don't we sit down and talk about it?" He gestured to the sofa.

Christian looked at the sofa for a very long time. He went to one of the chairs and settled himself there. Balthazar chuckled, but went to sit himself on the sofa.

"You *are* going to have to come near me to feed, fledgling," he said as he settled himself down, one arm stretched over the sofa's back and his legs indolently crossed.

"I will when the time comes." Christian regarded him coolly. "So you were going to tell me about feeding and sex."

"I'd rather show you."

"I'm sure you would." Christian's lips *almost* twitched into a smile.

"Vampires are all about pleasure. So yes, feeding and sex are intertwined. Feeding and violence are, too, as I said before," Balthazar answered. "Feeding from me–you won't be violent against your Master–will help you control your instinct later with others."

"Do you expect sex when I feed from you?"

To the point...

"I wouldn't mind it," Balthazar answered truthfully. Seeing no reaction from Christian, which made him think he should say more himself, Balthazar uncrossed and recrossed his legs, before expanding, "I don't *expect* anything. I will feed you no matter if you ever let me touch you in any other way. You are my fledgling. The question is really: do you want to?"

Christian swallowed.

"But nothing will happen unless *you* want it to happen," Balthazar assured him. "I take no pleasure in forcing myself on anyone. And I'll try not to be offended that you're worried about that."

"I don't know you," Christian answered softly. He leaned forward, elbows on his knees. "You don't seem like the type, but seeming and being are two different things."

"Have you..." Balthazar paused. He wasn't sure how to ask this or if he should. He wanted to know if Christian had been attacked. He knew that nothing had happened to the young man since he'd started watching over him. But that was only for the past eight years. Things could have happened *before* that. "Have you had *aggressive* people in your life?"

He nearly rolled his eyes. Christian was direct. But he couldn't quite make himself ask something so baldly.

"You're asking if I have *personal* reasons to distrust men?" This was as indirect as Christian had ever been.

"Yes."

"I don't trust anyone," Christian answered.

That was not an answer, but I will leave it for now.

"I will earn your trust, Christian," Balthazar promised.

Christian nodded, which showed neither belief nor disbelief. "So will you have sex with Sheila–"

"No," he laughed quietly.

"Why not?" Christian's eyes narrowed.

"She's a grandmotherly type," he answered.

"She's old?"

"She's sixty-seven," he answered.

Christian blinked. "I–I had this idea that you would only feed from nubile young men."

Balthazar snorted. "I do enjoy those types. For sure. But don't you like it when your mother makes you a meal? Isn't it comforting?"

"My mother is *not* my meal." Christian was giving him that very narrow eyed stare again.

He nodded. "No, but Sheila is loving, kind, gentle, tender and she's been doing this a long time for us. She knows what she's doing. So that will be a good thing for you."

"You want to sanitize the Vampire World for me. Why?"

"I'm not sanitizing it. I'm carefully *curating* it. Just at first. Believe me, you'll see much in a short time, but you're just beginning and things should be simpler," he told Christian.

In this age, people moved so quickly. Christian was a child of change. He was used to getting everything *now*. It was hard to explain–or maybe hard for him to understand–that he had eternity.

His fledgling was quiet for a moment, arms crossed over his chest, and eyes thoughtful. He nibbled his lower lip and glanced at Balthazar and then away then back again. Finally, Christian said, "You were willing to feed both Julian and me before you fed yourself. Can I... I feed from you for a moment now?"

Balthazar blinked. "Ah, yes, of course. If you wish..."

"Just a little. I'm just... I want to focus. And I *can't*. My thoughts are muddy," Christian admitted.

"I'm amazed at your strength so far." Balthazar's heart began to race. But he held himself very, very still again. "Do you want me to come to you or–"

"I'll come to you."

Christian came to his feet and Balthazar saw that his legs were trembling a little. Was it with fear or hunger or both?

A little bit of column A and a little bit of column B.

Christian stumbled as much as walked across the short distance between them and settled gracelessly on the couch by Balthazar's side. The Vampire Lord did not reach to steady him as much as he wanted to. And, oh, how much he wanted to. No, he stayed where he was and made no sudden movements.

When Christian was settled beside him, Balthazar turned his body towards the young man. His fledgling's breathing was raised and that high color was back on Christian's face. Christian's hands were on his lap, twitching rather nervously. Balthazar was nervous himself. This would be the first real feeding. Turning Christian was different. This would be the start of their relationship.

He extended his arm to undo the cufflinks at his wrist. Christian surprised him by taking his arm and doing it for him. Christian's long, elegant fingers quickly moved over his wrist as light as butterfly wings. His wrist and forearm were quickly exposed. Christian held his arm on his lap for long moments. Again, he forced himself not to talk or move. This was all for Christian. He had to make all the choices here. Christian's fingers were back on his skin. He was drawing them up and down along the soft flesh of his wrist and forearm up to his elbow.

"Your skin... it's different from human skin. Smoother. As if there are less pores or something. Mine isn't like that yet." Christian laid

41

one of his arms against Balthazar's to compare them. "Clearly, there are more changes in me to come."

"Yes, we do change with age. Normally, in good ways," Balthazar hardly trusted his voice to remain steady, but it did. Those teasing, teasing fingers!

Christian lifted Balthazar's bared wrist to his mouth. His light breath puffed against Balthazar's skin. He found himself leaning forward, wanting to see the moment that Christian's fangs came out and sank into his flesh.

His fledgling's lips drew back from his teeth and the fangs were out. Sharp and white and all new. Balthazar drew in a breath just as sharp. Christian's pink tongue slid out and licked his lips. His breathing was even faster now. Christian swallowed. His silver eyes were almost black with desire as he placed his teeth on Balthazar's wrist.

Those teeth pressed down. Balthazar felt the twin pricks of pain for just a moment before pleasure took over and he groaned. Blood burst like bright rubies and streamed down his wrist. But then Christian's lips fastened tightly over the twin wounds as he began to suck. Balthazar's fingers flexed and extended at every pull of that mouth on him. His heart beat matched the swallows. His cock stirred in his pants.

Color flooded Christian's face as Balthazar's blood surged through his new system. Pinpoints of sweat appeared on Christian's upper lip and sheened his forehead. His eyelids had shut tightly, fanning across the blushing cheeks.

He could feel Christian's mind so near his. He remembered this with Roan. His Master would force himself into Balthazar's mind and do what he wanted. But there was this moment when he was not alone and that had been good. He touched his mind to Christian's and he felt those pulls on his wrist *pause*.

I won't hurt you. I would never hurt you.

One of Christian's blond locks fell across his forehead as he continued to draw blood from Balthazar. The Vampire Lord couldn't resist using his fingers to move that lock back. Christian opened his eyes and met his gaze. His lips were suddenly away from Balthazar's wrist. The Vampire Lord wanted to object, but then Christian was kissing him.

Hot blood. Salt. Saliva. Teeth. Lips. Christian. Christian. Christian.

His fingers threaded through the hair at the back of Christian's head and held his fledgling to him. He wouldn't let go. He didn't want to let go. He *wouldn't* let go.

"So *this* is him," Rey's voice was dripping with hurt and anger. "The one you chose over me."

THE ART OF EVASION

*D*aemon watched his fledgling dress out of hooded eyes. The graceful sweep of Julian's spine as he bent over to pull on pants. The stretch and bunch of muscles under silken skin. The athletic grace that came from Julian's First Life as an explorer and, now, with Daemon's blood running through his veins, he was even more refined. Julian was in Balthazar's closet, choosing his outfit from the Eyros Vampire's clothing, which displeased Daemon. But Julian had explained that he had no choice.

"My own clothes are at my place," Julian had said. "I want to go back there, but with the Order and who knows who else is hunting us I don't think that's a good plan. At least not for now."

If they come to harm you, I will send them to their Second—and final—Deaths, Daemon had replied without hesitation. Because, of course, that would be *exactly* what he would do even faster than he had killed the other two in Nightvallen.

But his simple statement had caused no end of consternation in his fledgling, who had frozen at his words, only then to spring into frantic action. He'd come towards Daemon and gripped his biceps. His gaze was intense. It gave Daemon a chance to look carefully at Julian's eyes. He was pleased to see they held a purple cast. Close to

44

his red ones. Different from the other Vampires' silver orbs. It was yet one more thing to show that Julian was *his* fledgling, had *his* blood, and was *not* common.

"You can't just go around killing people," Julian informed him with all due seriousness. "The world is different now. And, anyways, killing is wrong. That's the first point."

This Daemon found most amusing, but he held his tongue. Killing was sometimes very *right*. But, from his surface perusal of Julian's mind, this age for his fledgling, at least, was incredibly peaceful. Violence was something that was done for entertainment. It was not real. Julian was much more interested in understanding someone's point of view than gutting them.

"Second, these are your people and they've been misled. So killing them is doubly wrong and won't win you friends," Julian continued.

This had some merit. It appeared that the Vampires had been led astray. The Immortals may have violated his laws while he slept, creating chaos and dysfunction in this world. He would be looking into this and fixing what was broken. It disturbed him that he could not sense the other Immortals. Death was not a possibility. Not in the way that Julian understood it. Was he so weak that he was cut off from them? Or were they so damaged that they could not reach back? Or there was the possibility that they were simply hiding. He did not know what disturbed him more.

"Third," Julian further continued, "clothes are *not* worthy of killing anyone over. Even if it means that I have to wear Balthazar's clothes. Besides, he's fussy and territorial. I think wearing his stuff might annoy him. You like doing that."

The last had been said with a grin. His activities with the cologne and the toilet had not been forgotten.

Daemon snorted. *Wearing his things makes you smell like him. It displeases me.*

"Well, you're going to have to be displeased. In fact, you might need to wear some of his things yourself. Though," Julian frowned as he measured Daemon with his eyes, "I don't know if they'd fit you. Maybe some of Arcius' stuff would be big enough though he's nowhere near as tall as you. Though I guess what you have on now will do since we're just going to be hanging out inside the house."

Daemon looked down at his bare chest, black leather trousers and thigh-high leather boots. His wolf's fur coat was on the bed.

What is wrong with what I'm wearing?

It was Julian's turn to snort. "The fact that you have to ask tells me that you have no idea what the current styles are."

Daemon frowned. He picked up the wolf's fur coat and slipped it on.

My style is eternal.

Julian really laughed then, which had him smiling, too. Julian's laughter had the immediate effect of warming.

"Yeah, it is. It screams Vampire King or member of a really interesting rock band," Julian chuckled. "From what I saw of your wardrobe in the Ever Dark, we'll definitely have to buy you clothes so you'll fit in here."

We cannot go back to Nightvallen for some time.

Daemon tried not to sound sad about that. Coming for Julian was nothing he would ever regret.

Concerned lines appeared on Julian's forehead. "Why? I mean, I'm guessing it would take too much energy for you to create a doorway again like you did to get here, but what about the library? Can't we use the way Christian and I got in?"

Yes, but my body needs to stabilize. One place or the other. Not passing between both continuously, he explained.

Julian thought about this for a moment, but then nodded, understanding it not completely, but enough. "Okay, so we definitely don't go out looking for clothes or things we don't really need. Not until you're much stronger." Julian frowned then. "Before you came, I was really weak. I felt like I couldn't even get up from the bed. But you haven't fed me and I feel okay now, good even. Why is that?"

My presence alone has given you strength. But I must feed you soon or you will start to regress again, Daemon guessed.

If Julian was like other fledglings that would be the case. But Julian was singular. No one knew how he would react. *And what if taking in more of my blood harms him?* But Daemon didn't allow himself to think about that too long or seriously. He would feed his fledgling. No one else would have that honor.

"Oh, well, cool. We need to keep a low profile and not endanger House Ravenscroft in any case. So staying here and feeding is the plan," Julian answered.

Did Balthazar truly convince a whole room full of Vampires to freeze and then wipe their minds? he asked again.

Julian had informed him of everything that had occurred since their connection had been severed. He'd thought that Julian had died when that happened. But clearly not. Thinking of Julian dying made him feel strangely fragile. Shudders ran through him and his mind seemed to want to freeze at it. He pushed it away from himself. Julian was here. Julian was his. Those things would *remain*. He willed it.

As to why their mental link had failed when Julian went into Siryn territory, he believed now that it was because the other Immortals had locked their worlds down, which partially kept him out, though Julian had still been able to pass into the Blood Den. He would have to grow stronger to reach out to them if they were still on this plane or simply rip the locks off if they were not.

"Yeah, it was pretty epic," Julian said and there was awe in his eyes.

I suppose I should be grateful that his show of power made you think him worthy of drinking from, Daemon finally answered.

Julian grinned and shook his head. "Well, it's not connecting two worlds or becoming an army of wolves. But I think it was impressive nonetheless."

Daemon's lips curled into a smile. *Yes, but definitely not on the same level.*

"No, but you've got to give him credit. Actually, I think you *do*. You're surprised that Balthazar could do that," Julian pointed out.

Daemon grimaced slightly. *I can tell he is young. It is unusual. He interests me... on a very superficial level.*

"You shouldn't be mad at him. He didn't really believe in you.

Maybe still doesn't. Not yet anyways. But he helped Christian and would've helped me, too," Julian pointed out.

Helped himself to you. You wish me to be impressed by the fact that he tried to steal you from me. It shows he has good taste, but little sense. Daemon had crossed his arms over his chest defensively and, upon realizing this, he dropped them to his sides. *I did not kill him. That is enough of a reward.*

"You and the killing." Julian shook his head. "I would have thought that living forever would make you respect life before. You must *love* to live."

I do, but I am a predator. Life is what I feed upon. Life is what I need to keep going. Other people's lives. You will understand that soon, too, I think, Daemon had told him.

Julian didn't look convinced, but said, "Maybe. I don't know that I *want* to feel that way. Or, at least, not be so cavalier about it."

We shall see.

"All set to go, I think," Julian's voice stirred him from his reverie.

He was disappointed to see that all that supple, silky skin was covered up again and he'd missed seeing the last of it disappear as he'd ruminated on their earlier conversation. Julian seemed to favor loose, baggy clothing that hid his muscular form in drab colors. Not that Julian wasn't beautiful in even these strange, utilitarian outfits. He *was*. It was just that he should be seen in silk, furs and leather to be truly arrayed properly.

Currently, Julian was wearing some black cotton pants with a drawstring waist and a long sleeved dune-colored shirt. He'd also grabbed a pair of shoes that were slip-ons in an almost matching color to the shirt. He was running his fingers through his still damp hair to arrange it. Daemon stepped forward and knocked his hands away gently so that he could rearrange the strands.

"Making a mess of it, was I?" Julian asked with a rather puckish smile.

You take no pride in your beauty. That was a statement more than a question.

"I guess. It's never held me back." Julian shrugged.

I suppose I should be grateful. You would have already had a suitor if you had presented yourself in a truly optimal light, Daemon murmured.

Julian's eyebrows rose up and a smile twitched his lips. "I've had suitors. *Tons of suitors.* I'm just not dating anyone right now, because I don't want to. But I *could* get someone even without brushing my hair."

Daemon's eyes narrowed. *I see.*

"I bet you've had lots of suitors." Julian stood still while Daemon carded his fingers through those soft dark strands.

Of course.

"Of course?" Julian laughed again, delighted.

Do you not think I am worthy of such? He imitated affront with a stiffening spine and raised eyebrow.

Though Julian could not read his thoughts fully, the young man knew he was teasing. "Oh, undoubtedly. Actually, I'm sure you have." He shifted uncomfortably. "Which makes me want to ask... Does the fledgling/Master relationship mean we're exclusive to one another?"

Daemon sifted through Julian's mind to understand the context he was truly speaking of. Julian's thoughts were fascinating. They showed him two bodies intertwined then the symbol of rings then two lights becoming one. Images of his parents floated through his mind. Memories of them laughing, of them holding one another, of how his father would simply rest his head against his mother's and they would stay that way, silent yet serene, for long moments.

Soul mates.

"What?" Julian hadn't heard him fully. Those were the words, the *idea*, that Julian had about exclusivity.

Some have been... exclusive, Daemon answered carefully. *Some have not.*

"So it's not some automatic thing, which is good. I was just wondering. I feel..." Julian licked his upper lip as he debated saying what he was feeling. "*Connected* to you. It's what I imagined..." *My parents felt.* But he did not say that or send that to Daemon consciously. "It's just an interesting feeling."

Conflicting, too? Daemon's right eyebrow rose.

A flustered movement of Julian's left hand had Daemon gently clasping it.

"You shouldn't do that," Julian said with a slight frown upon plush lips.

Do what?

"Read more of my thoughts than I want you to." And with a faint smile, he added, "And I know you know how much I want read."

I do. Sometimes. Other times, it seems you both do and do not want me to delve deeper. Daemon drew his thumb along the hand he still held.

"Well, like I said, I'm glad that it's not automatic. We need to get to know one another, and, kisses in the shower notwithstanding," another flash of a smile, "we're practically strangers to one another."

And that matters?

Julian sent him a sharp look. "Doesn't it matter to you? Or are you just ready to jump feet first into whatever this is?"

What did he feel? Only one single line came to him and he sent it, *You are mine.*

Daemon then turned away from Julian and headed to the door of the bedroom. He knew that wasn't an answer and that was likely going to cause the very independent Julian to squawk. But he couldn't answer more than that. His feelings were *complex*.

He had not sorted them out yet. The truth was that the thought of Julian being with anyone else made him see red. He'd never been possessive of his lovers before. It made little sense to do so when eternity–and an infinite number of experiences–beckoned. There were those who were always by one's side, but variety and interests were to be pursued. But with Julian things were different. He needed time to figure out that difference.

Julian's footsteps as he jogged up behind him and the not unexpected question came quickly, "What does that mean?"

I need to eat.

A strangled laugh came from Julian. "Okaaaaay. Evidently, we're not talking about this subject. Or, at least, *you* aren't talking. But since I have a say in this, why don't I tell you what I think? What I want? At least for now."

Daemon's steps as he strode down the hallway, towards the scent of fresh blood, slightly hitched. What if Julian said that he didn't wish to be exclusive? What if he said he did not want more than the kiss they'd had in the shower? What if...

Daemon stopped abruptly in the middle of the hallway and spun around to face his fledgling, who nearly barreled into him, but his Vampire reflexes caught him at the last moment from doing so.

"Uhm... you okay?" Julian asked, tilting his head to the side.

You are having more of an effect on me than I realized.

Daemon slowly studied Julian's hair. The thick hair. The lush lashes that would have made him pretty except for the masculine beard. The strong jaw. The swanlike neck. The thud of that heart he already had memorized like it was his own.

"How so?" Another frown. Julian was frowning much too much for his liking.

Your quick, mortal thinking is trying to rush me into discussing something that neither of us is prepared to answer at this time. Daemon paused and considered his fledgling further. He wanted to map Julian's body with his hands and his mouth. He wanted to know what he smelled like when fully aroused and then spent. He wanted to see every one of his smiles. He wanted... *Would you have me command you to be only mine? If I say this, as your Master, as your king, it means something more than you realize. You think this is just a conversation between us, but it is not.*

And it was not a conversation that he'd really ever expected to have. The fledglings he'd tried to make before had died so terribly. He'd kept himself apart from them during the whole process. But with Julian? Julian had been *inside* of him from the beginning despite his best efforts to stay away. Julian challenged his need to protect himself from the pain of separation with the equally powerfully duty of honor.

Those potential fledglings that had come to him before, had always done so with awe and gratitude. He was the First Among Equals. The king. That was not how he and Julian had met. They had met as two people, two individuals. Julian saw him as powerful, but there was no worship there. Julian saw them as *equals*.

So he was not at all surprised when Julian said, "I don't believe in Masters or kings, Daemon. You're a *person* to me. An individual. Not an institution. I do what I want. I do what's best for me. And you. Of course, you, too."

He brushed his fingers down Julian's cheek. *The fact that you say this, tells me that you truly do not understand. I am more than just an Immortal. I am the king. And are my fledgling. My one... and perhaps only one. Forever.*

"Do you want other fledglings?" Julian's eyes burned red for a moment. Jealousy was not just in Daemon's breast, evidently. This shouldn't please him too much, but it did. His fledgling's emotions were quick, too. Like a lit match.

He is not yet sure of me. Can I blame him? But he said only, *Handling one of you is a trial. I cannot imagine more.* But Julian kept that hard, red stare on him so he went on, *You are the only one that has ever survived. I do not know why. But I think it is Fate. I would not press Fate for another gift such as you.*

"But you *want* another fledgling?" Julian pushed.

He feathered his hands through the hair at the back of Julian's head. So soft. *I want only you.*

He kissed Julian. At first, his fledgling's lips were resistant to his, not conceding, not allowing pleasure and tenderness to flow between them. But slowly they softened and Julian's hands were fisted in his coat's fur. His fledgling was breathing heavily when they broke apart.

"It's like a rollercoaster being with you, Daemon. I feel so out of control." Julian's mouth formed a pained smile. "Sometimes that's good. You know? When you just let go and jump off that cliff? Sometimes there's a pool of clear water below you, but other times there are jagged rocks. Not knowing is part of the *thrill* that keeps me jumping. But this... it feels like you have my heart in your hands even though..."

He shook his head and stepped back from Daemon. The slight

physical distance between them was agony. Daemon reached for Julian, but the young man slid out of reach. He shook his head again.

"Daemon, when you touch me, everything in my head short circuits. I want to be *clear* for this conversation," Julian explained.

There can be no conversation—

"Why?" Julian's head snapped up, staring at him again with flaring red eyes. "Does what I want not matter?"

It matters. It matters very much. But, like you, I am out of control. I am riding on this need to just... His hand that was still outstretched towards Julian curled into a fist. *You are mine. I am yours. And this is dangerous.*

Julian's voice was but a whisper, "Why dangerous?"

Because my instincts are urging me to take you away from everyone and everything. To destroy any who would come near you. You think killing is wrong. Killing is what I do. And you would see it. Rivers of blood... Daemon shuddered and stopped. That had happened before. When he'd lost control. After a beloved potential fledgling had died and he had... *Turned everything to a red mist.*

Julian's expression wasn't horrified. Not exactly. It was a mixture of many things which was reflected in his next words, "I don't know whether to feel treasured or scared as hell."

Both. Daemon dropped his hand to his side. *You are brave and independent. I would not change that in you. Not the better part of me anyways. But the other part? The other part wants to keep you for myself and only myself.*

Julian crossed his arms over his chest. "Funny, I feel the same way about you. Only I wouldn't be killing people to make that happen. Only kicking things. Punching walls, maybe."

And the moment he said it, Daemon found himself laughing, out loud, which had a startling effect on both of them. Julian jerked back and then grinned. Daemon had not heard himself laugh in a long time either.

"So you can make noise! I was beginning to wonder! Though why are you laughing?"

I can make noise if I wish. And I am laughing, because you are so exactly like what I need, but nothing like what I thought you'd be, Daemon admitted.

"You're just used to being in charge and so am I. We're both alphas." Julian grinned at him wider.

Alphas? I see. I suppose I would expect no less from my fledgling. He would have to be a leader. Daemon leaned towards Julian. *But I am in charge between us.*

He knew that Julian would perk up at the challenge and he did. "We'll have to see about that!"

They turned and began to companionably make their way up the stairs to the first floor, teasing one another about who would be in charge, when Daemon's hearing tuned into the voices of other Vampires in the house. He put a hand out in front of Julian to stop his forward progress. Both of them listened.

A woman was saying, "Arcius, why didn't Balthazar consult us after this–this *person* entered our home? I understand that he is distracted by his new fledgling, but this is madness!"

"This *person* is our king," Arcius was explaining patiently, but his tone indicated that he had been saying this *repeatedly*.

"That's insane!" A high, boyish voice cried out. "Daemon is a myth! I'm sorry, Arcius, but I think your faith is blinding you to what has to be a fraud!"

"Worse than a fraud!" the woman got in. "The Order clearly has some beef with this person. We don't need that kind of attention. Our House has just now started to establish itself. All of that could be lost by taking in this–this con man!"

"Why are you so certain he is false?" Arcius' tone was even, the tone of a person used to being doubted, but knowing he knew the truth nonetheless. "You have not even met him."

"Nothing he says or does will convince us that he's *really* King Daemon," the boy answered for her.

Daemon's eyes narrowed. Nothing would convince them, would it? Nothing at all? He would make them eat those words. Julian's hand was suddenly gripping his shoulder. He turned to his fledgling.

Julian's expression was firm as he said, "No killing, Daemon. Remember that they are our *allies*."

Do not worry, my fledgling. Daemon smiled mirthlessly. *I would not be able to enjoy them admitting how very wrong they were to doubt me if I killed them.*

He swept up the stairs to meet the Vampires who doubted his existence.

RESPECT

❧

"Rey, you shouldn't be here," Balthazar said and, while his voice wasn't angry exactly, it was *crisp*.

Christian saw a young man–blond like him with sky blue eyes and pouty lips–react to it. Those slender, but muscular shoulders curled inwards and an almost *guilty* look crossed his fox-like features. But then Rey shook off whatever he was feeling at that tone and allowed his anger to rise again like a phoenix.

"He looks like me!" Rey spat as he narrowed his eyes at Christian.

"Actually, *you* look like *him*," Balthazar murmured with a rather guilty glance at Christian.

Christian–who was still in the Vampire Lord's arms–stiffened at that confession. Balthazar had been fantasizing about him with this Rey for who knew how long. And Christian hadn't even known that the Vampire Lord existed!

Christian knew that this fear of being thought of by those who he didn't know was foolish. He and Julian had a very successful web series. Tons of people thought of him and he didn't know them and likely would never know them.

It's because this reminds me of David watching me, stalking me. That's why Balthazar unnerves me. But he isn't David. He's nothing like him. That

56

he admired me before we met doesn't put them at all in the same category. My reaction is not logical. It's atavistic. I will conquer it.

Balthazar slowly drew a hand down Christian's spine to comfort him, but Christian wanted to be free. He pulled back. Balthazar immediately released him. There wasn't the slightest use of that great strength to hold him near even though he knew that Balthazar was hurt by his drawing back.

Not like David, see? Not going to hold me against my will. Not going to... Everything is fine. Fine. Fine.

The tightness in Christian's chest eased as he settled himself on the couch on a separate cushion from the Vampire Lord. He needed space. He needed distance. He needed to calm down and force reason upon his emotions. He found himself licking at the little bit of blood still on his lips from their feeding. That taste actually made him feel better. Actually, it made him feel *safe*.

Rey smirked. "Well, it appears that the only thing similar about us is looks. I've never been so bashful about being seen in an embrace with you, Balthazar. Far more than that. We've fucked in front of an audience dozens of times. I bet he won't even let you hold his hand–"

"Enough, Rey," Balthazar's voice was ice and the note of command was in the air as well. Christian recognized it from the Blood Den.

Rey immediately went silent. But more than that, his face went blank. He stood there like an empty-headed doll. Christian's gaze snapped to the Vampire Lord. Balthazar squeezed the top of his nose and murmured something in what sounded like French. Finally, he lowered his hand and, though he looked as beautiful as ever, he appeared tired and sad.

"I'm sorry about that, Christian. He shouldn't have been allowed up here, let alone to say such things. I will fix this. I won't be gone for a moment." Balthazar stood up.

Christian grasped his wrist gently. "What are you going to do?" Without waiting for an answer he plowed on, "You're going to wipe his mind, aren't you?"

That tired, sad look became more apparent on Balthazar's handsome visage. Christian found himself liking the Vampire Lord a lot for that look. Rey seemed like an asshole, but that rudeness towards Christian had come from hurt. Still, even if it hadn't, Christian wouldn't have wanted someone's mind to be wiped just because they were a jerk.

"Yes, Christian. I must do it. Remember those boundaries I talked about between a Vampire and an Acolyte? I crossed them with Rey because..." Balthazar's lips flattened and Christian could tell that the Vampire Lord didn't want to tell him why, was considering lying, but tossed that away, too.

"Because he looks like me?" Christian guessed.

One of Balthazar's eyebrows raised. "Yes, pet, because he looks like you."

"You are not calling me 'pet'." Christian scowled.

An impish smile quirked the corners of Balthazar's lips. "Oh? I don't know. I rather like—"

"Seriously, Balthazar, what will happen to Rey?" Christian insisted and lightly squeezed Balthazar's wrist.

It was the same wrist he had drunk from and then, in a fit of madness, had kissed Balthazar afterwards. What had possessed him to do that? But just as he realized that David was the cause of him shying away from Balthazar, his body, at least, had no problem desiring the Vampire Lord. It was more honest than his mind was at times.

The Vampire Lord sighed. "He will be given false memories of traveling the world. His social media has been reflecting this fake life for the whole time he's been here. He'll have lots of experiences and do-gooding on his resume. He will be offered a prestigious job by another of our Acolytes in another city very far away from here. He will be happy and content and never know the truth."

Christian considered this. Rey was being "paid" for his time with a good career and pleasant memories. He would never regret losing what he didn't remember.

"But it's all a lie. The most important things to ever happen to him—the knowledge that supernatural, immortal beings exist and the fact that he *loved* one of them—will be erased," Christian whispered. "It's... it's terrible."

"And necessary." Another sigh and squeeze of the top of his nose. "You have to understand, Christian, that not every Acolyte can be turned into a Vampire. First, it would mean too many of us. Second, not all are suited to eternity. The things that make someone a good Acolyte don't translate to being a good Vampire. Believe me when I tell you that Rey would *never* have been turned with or without this display tonight."

"Why not?"

If it was possible, Balthazar looked more exhausted. His shoulders slumped. "We can tell what personality types will thrive as Vampires and which will be problematic. Some of the things that made Rey... well, *Rey*, would make him likely to go out of control as a Vampire. He leaps before he looks and overshares. He pushes boundaries, not in good ways, but in ways that would break the very rules that keep Vampires safe. If he were turned, I am almost certain he would have been put down in the end."

Christian stiffened. "Put down? You mean killed?" A nod from Balthazar had Christian staring into those blank, doll-like eyes of Rey. "So some fake memories and a job are better options."

"Yes."

"I'm sorry," Christian said finally.

Balthazar's brow furrowed. "For what? You aren't responsible for this."

"For not realizing how hard this is for you. Earlier, I acted like you were being cavalier with people. I can see that's not true now," Christian admitted. "I can see doing this hurts you."

Balthazar dipped his head back and stared up at the ceiling. "You shouldn't feel sorry for me, Christian. This was my fault. I allowed the lines to be crossed, because I really wanted you and Rey was a convenient substitute. Rey is nothing like you, ironically. But he semi-satisfied an *itch* I had and now... this is the price for it. We lose a good Acolyte."

"So you really didn't want Selene to hurt Julian or me?" Christian asked. Not that he had disbelieved Balthazar about this earlier, but it was utterly clear to him now how her actions were completely against Balthazar's wishes.

"God, no. I have no idea why she and Heath did that. Selene's Master—Timothy—has disappeared and Elena is, as you know, unconscious. But there is more here than just two Acolytes going beyond what I asked of them," Balthazar answered and his expression darkened. "I have a bad feeling that I've been *betrayed*."

Christian resisted the urge to apologize again. It wasn't logical to do so. Yet he found himself not wanting to see Balthazar upset.

Likely part of the Master-fledgling bond and yet I do not feel compelled in any way to care for him. So maybe I just feel badly for him naturally.

"Our House is exiled, Christian. If we cannot trust one another then... then there is simply nothing left," Balthazar explained.

At that moment, there was the sound of the patter of footsteps coming up the stairs and a frantic Laura appeared in the doorway. She saw Rey and looked startled at his presence and the blank look on his face, but that clearly wasn't what was bringing her to them and causing her such great distress.

"What is it, Laura?" Balthazar commanded.

"There's a fight! A fight in the main house!" she cried.

Christian was off of the couch. His hearing had suddenly become exquisitely sensitive and he could hear Julian demanding someone *not* touch another person.

"Daemon. Julian," Christian said. "They're being attacked!"

"Damnit!"

Balthazar and he ran out of the room, leaving Laura and Rey behind. He hoped they wouldn't be too late to stop whatever was happening in the main house.

***

Earlier ...

Julian had to practically run after Daemon. The Vampire King swept up the stairs, his long flowing fur coat spreading out behind him like a pair of wings. The three Vampires that had been speaking about him went silent as soon as Daemon appeared.

Arcius immediately bowed low while the other two looked at Daemon out of narrowed eyes. One was a young man who looked hardly older than thirteen with hair so pale it was almost white. In contrast, the woman beside him had hair as black as a raven's wing with a matching form-fitting dress and a choker of pearls around her swanlike throat.

"My king! Julian! I did not expect you to be here!" Arcius' surprise could not be hidden. That was understandable. He had left them with Daemon, unconscious, on the bed, and Julian weak as a kitten. Yet here they both were in good health.

Julian's stomach clenched a little with hunger pangs though. He really needed to eat or he'd be in a bad state. Daemon's head swung towards him. But Julian made a small movement with his hand. He was fine. For now. They didn't have to rush off. Though *maybe* he should have suggested that, considering the looks that the boy and woman were giving them.

"Hey, Arcius, we were just heading to get some *food*." Julian winced a little at calling people food. "Could you maybe point the way?"

The idea of Daemon proving to these angry, nettled Vampires he was their king, suddenly seemed like a very bad idea. Distracting Daemon with food was the much better course.

Daemon inclined his head and Arcius straightened up from his bow. "Of–of course. I would be honored to take you to the coach house–"

"You're going to let them *feed* on our Acolytes?" It was the woman who spoke. She sounded outraged.

Arcius kept his tone level and even as he answered her, "Of course, Isabel. These are Balthazar's guests, regardless of what else you may be thinking."

"Balthazar is treating the Vampire con-artist who killed Selene and Heath like a guest? Has he lost his mind?" It was the boy who spoke.

"William!" Arcius' voice was tinged with outrage. His gaze flickered between the white haired boy and Daemon. He knew that these words were meant to offend and, clearly, he had no doubt that they would be answered by the Vampire King with violence. Remembering how easily Daemon killed, Julian totally agreed with his assess-ment. "Hold your tongue! You are out of line!"

Daemon, surprisingly, said and did nothing. After his appearance as a horde of wolves before, Julian had expected him to do something dramatic or just snap William's neck like a twig and walk on. But he was simply observing everything and everyone. Unlike Arcius, he didn't appear moved at all by William's anger.

William stepped over to Daemon on slender legs. The boy–for he was a *boy*–was thin as a rail. He looked like a strong wind could push him over. But he went right up to the Vampire King without fear, an angry, predatory light in his silver eyes. He was over a foot shorter than Daemon and had to tip his head back to meet the Vampire King's gaze. Yet the difference in their sizes didn't daunt him at all.

"You killed Heath. You killed Selene. They were my friends. My *family*. You have devastated Elena and we cannot even find Timothy. He's likely stricken down somewhere. Perhaps having suffered his Second Death, too. That is four people in our House you have harmed," William's voice was arctic. "Balthazar wants us to treat you as a guest? I cannot do this. Even if you were the legendary *king* of all Vampires, I would want you *dead*."

In a movement so fast, Julian didn't even see it happening, William's right hand shot for Daemon's throat. But he didn't make it there. Only it wasn't Daemon who had stopped him. It was *Julian*.

Julian found his hand was wrapped around William's right wrist, holding it in place, with seeming ease. He hadn't even realized he'd done it. It was like his body knew what was coming from William even as his mind struggled to keep up. No other Vampire had made a move. Daemon hadn't even blinked. It was as if he had expected this to happen all along.

"Don't touch him," Julian found himself saying. "Don't you dare touch him. If you wish to blame someone for Selene and Heath's deaths then you need to blame *me*. I asked Daemon to kill them. They were trying to kill Christian and I *first*. It was self-defense. But I am the one *ultimately* responsible for them dying."

"Then *you* will die, too!"   William hissed and wrenched his arm away from Julian.

The child-like Vampire was set to strike out again. Arcius bellowed for him to stop and made a move to wrap his bearlike arms around the boy who seemed to be all muscle. But there was no need. William was suddenly floating in mid air. His eyes went wide. He clawed at the air with his hands and kicked at it with his feet, trying to get purchase, but he was as harmless as a kitten.

"Ashyr Bloodline. Telekinesis," Isabel murmured.

It was only then that he noted her fingernails had seemingly grown into claws, but she didn't look like she was going to use them. Her eyes were huge with shock. Daemon tilted his head to the side as he moved his right hand in the air, which, in turn moved William until the young man was floating on his stomach at his eye level. William had stopped hissing and spitting. He didn't look as brave as he had before. There was a hint of fear in those silver eyes. But he did not beg for his life. Julian had to give him credit for that. He would have personally been peeing himself a little if Daemon looked at him with such an outright *alien* stare.

There was the thump of many feet and the rush of clothing. Over a dozen Vampires appeared in all of the doorways. There was no way out of that room that wasn't filled with enemies. Julian's heart beat hard. Fangs and claws were exposed. Silver eyes, shining in the dark, were fixed upon them. The Vampires started to advance.

"People, you need to all disperse!" Arcius waved a hand towards the Vampires. But it did no good. They continued to move in.

Stop.

One word. Just like Balthazar, except it felt more *primal.* It felt like that word settled in Julian's bones. Imprinted there. He felt that if Daemon had meant it to be more than simply stop moving that it could have stopped all their hearts and breathing and their very *existence.*

"Eyros Bloodline. Mind control," Isabel croaked.

Arcius cleared his throat, awe written on his face even though he had already accepted Daemon as their king. "All of you need to leave. Balthazar will explain—"

"Let them stay," Daemon said. Out loud.

His voice was rich and rolling. There was something of a mid-Atlantic accent about it or maybe French or maybe German or... it was like nothing on this Earth. It was *beautiful* though and it *commanded*. It was like hearing *music*.

"Siryn Bloodline. Song compulsion," Isabel murmured. Her claws and fangs had fully retracted. Her arms hung limply at her sides. "The First Among Equals is said to have the powers of all other Bloodlines and—"

"Armageddon," Arcius whispered. There was fear in the Confessor's eyes. He was clearly worried that Daemon might inflict that on all of them.

No killing, Daemon. Please, Julian begged silently, but he knew the Vampire King had heard him. There was the softest mental caresses in response.

"They must see and understand," Daemon continued in that musical yet deadly voice.

He slowly began to walk around the room, regarding each and every Vampire in it. As he met each Vampire's gaze, they lowered theirs, unable to win a staredown with him. Many actually bowed their heads.

William continued to hang in the air like some very bizarre light fixture. Arcius and Isabel stayed where they were. It took a moment for Julian to shake off the compulsion to stay and instead he went to Daemon's side. He kept slightly behind him and to the side of the Vampire King. He would defend him, like he had against William, if any of the Vampires attacked.

He doesn't need any protection! Isn't he showing that to them now? But Julian had no intention of being away from him.

Finally, they finished their circuit of the room and returned to William. Though he looked at William as he spoke, Daemon was addressing all in that room, "I sent Selene and Heath to their Second Deaths. Julian asked me to do it, but I would have done so in any case.

They came to Nightvallen *uninvited*. They sought to kill the one that would become my first *fledgling*. Second Deaths have been earned for far less from me."

Julian was shocked to see tears spring into William's eyes. He looked so like a beautiful child that it was painful to see. Like a little boy about to dissolve into tears for lost friends.

"What's going on here?!" It was Balthazar's voice which rose up at that moment. He and Christian pushed through the Vampires and came towards them.

Christian made a beeline for Julian. They embraced.

"Are you okay?" Christian's voice was blurred against Julian's shoulder.

"I'm fine. Just a little *issue* about those two Vampires that attacked us in Nightvallen," he explained.

Christian pulled back and looked at the floating William. His best friend put it all together in an instant. "He went after Daemon and you for it?"

"Yeah. The Vampires were his friends," Julian answered.

Balthazar's face reddened with rage as he heard this. His silver eyes *burned*. He grasped William's chin cruelly. "You attacked my guests?"

William's already porcelain pale face went a gray color. He opened trembling lips and stammered, "He–he *killed* Heath and Selene!"

"Because they fucking disobeyed *my* orders and went into goddamned Nightvallen!" Balthazar roared. "They tried to kill Christian and Julian! If Daemon hadn't killed them, I would have!" Those words echoed throughout the room. Balthazar's head snapped towards all of his Vampires. "You've embarrassed me. You've shamed me. You've disobeyed me. I don't compel you! I give you freedom. I listen to all your goddamned complaints. But what do I get in return? Betrayal. Disrespect. Am I your lord or not? Any who think I am not worthy of leading you, speak up now! I'll have no problem showing you the old ways! Do you want that? Are we going back to that?"

None challenged him. Heads hung low. Shame practically radiated off of the group, excluding Julian, Christian, Daemon and Arcius.

"You are my lord, Balthazar!" William sobbed. "I'm sorry! I—"

Balthazar's hand tightened so much on his chin that Julian swore he heard the bones *creak*. "Don't. Don't speak. Don't even—"

"He's going to kill him," Julian whispered in horror. "Christian, I don't want this!"

"Please don't kill him, Balthazar." Christian stepped up by William's side so that he was in Balthazar's line of sight.

Balthazar's handsome face tightened. "Christian, I know you don't like violence, but this—"

"Isn't necessary," Christian insisted, his voice calm and even. "He acted out of love and pain. It's clear he didn't mean to disrespect you and, it's equally clear, he couldn't have done anything to Daemon or Julian."

"I didn't mean it! I love you, my lord!" William bleated.

Balthazar's jaw clenched. His head turned slightly towards Daemon. "You are the wronged party, Daemon. What would you ask of me? If it is his death, it shall happen."

Please, Daemon, no. This is Christian's new House. I want us to be a part of it, too. We can't do that with all this death, Julian begged.

"I require nothing more of you than what you have already done," Daemon answered and William was set upon the ground. The boy Vampire immediately fell to his knees before Balthazar. "His desire to avenge his friends' deaths is commendable." Daemon spread his arms towards the other Vampires in the room. "The fact that your House came to his defense without hesitation speaks well of them and of *you*, Lord Balthazar. You have forged a family among people who have been cast out and ill-used. I am sorry to have taken any of them from you."

Julian's eyes closed a moment as he murmured, *Thank you, Daemon.*

He opened his eyes to see Balthazar's reaction to Daemon actually *speaking*, not to mention what he had said. Balthazar had frozen. But then he slowly, almost haltingly, turned his head to fully face the Vampire King. For one moment, Julian could see this raw wound that was exposed and a wild, almost shocked hope in Balthazar's expression. The look was gone as fast as it had appeared. Balthazar blinked and went back to looking down at William, though he didn't really seem to be seeing the other Vampire.

"I–I appreciate your... your *kind* words, Daemon." His voice rose as he addressed the rest of his house, "Daemon and Julian are my guests. You will treat them as you would any other member of this House. Do you understand me?"

There were murmured assents all around. Silence fell once again.

"Arcius, you were going to take us to where we might feed?" Daemon asked the Confessor.

Arcius' head snapped up and his mouth opened and closed rather fishlike for a moment, but then he said graciously, "Of course. Let me take you there now."

Daemon held out a hand towards Julian without turning to look at him. Julian cast a glance at Christian, but his best friend urged him to go with a nod of his head. He would take care of Balthazar and the aftermath of this mess.

Julian grasped Daemon's hand and they followed Arcius out of the room. The other Vampires parted before them with bowed heads and averted eyes.

Never a dull moment with you, is there? Julian asked Daemon.

The Vampire King flashed him a smile. *Never indeed.*

ON RAVEN'S WINGS

*J*ulian felt fine tremors running through Daemon's hand in his. He gently rubbed his thumb against the back of that shaking hand while they followed Arcius through the house.

As Arcius spoke on the phone to Acolytes in the coach house about preparing for their arrival, Julian thought of how the Vampire King had been so nonchalant about using his powers. But Julian knew now that it had strained Daemon's already depleted energy reserves potentially to their breaking point. Julian covered their clasped hands with his free one and squeezed, willing his own strength into Immortal. The Vampire King looked down at him with a mixed look of surprise and pleasure, but also with some *consternation*.

I don't think anyone else can tell how exhausted you are, Julian sent.

A faint frown appeared on Daemon's plush lips. *You should not be taking care of me. I should be taking care of you. I am the Master. I am the king. I am the one that you should lean on. Not the other way around.*

Julian suppressed a sigh and shook his head. *I'm not some damsel in distress and neither are you. We should be leaning on each other. Like partners. And tonight, you need a little help. You cannot deny that.*

Though Daemon did not respond to this, at first, Julian sensed the

Vampire King's dissatisfaction with it. He didn't think it stemmed from any idea of superiority exactly. It was Daemon's view of himself as the king, the First Among Equals, the protector, the warrior, and the one to be taking on the challenges everyone else fled from.

After I feed and rest, I shall be myself again, Daemon finally answered.

And, until you are, I'll be right beside you. Just like I was when William tried ripping your throat out. Julian could still feel the iron grip he'd held William's wrist in.

This time Daemon grinned. *You are quite pleased with yourself about that.*

Hell, yes! I didn't even think about doing it. It just happened all on its own. I was a badass. Julian grinned back.

You were much stronger and faster than he was. He will consider this fact later that one so young as you—who has not fed—was able to stop him.

You didn't seem surprised that I did that, Julian pointed out.

He'd wondered why that was. If his reflexes were lightning quick then Daemon's had to be double that so the Vampire King could have blocked William even before he had.

Daemon shrugged. *I was not. You are my fledgling. Of course, you would be stronger and faster than any other here. So I knew you could take him and that would allow you to start to garner respect.*

Julian snorted. *Why does it seem like you're saying that YOU are the only reason I won?*

Because it is. My blood makes you strong.

Julian raised his eyebrows, but Daemon's expression was serene. He had no compunctions about believing in his superiority. Thinking on how easily he handled William and all the Vampires, maybe he was right.

Daemon continued, *But you survived my blood. No one else has. So there is something inherent in you that allows you to accept such strength.*

Might doesn't always equal right, you know? People shouldn't be picked to lead solely because they are strong, Julian argued.

You are correct. I am far more than just stronger than all others, Daemon answered magnanimously.

Julian let out a soft guffaw. *Okay, okay, I see how it is. You're perfect.*

No, I am the king, Daemon answered solemnly. *I must be more so I have made myself more. You will see.*

They passed out of the house now and were following a path through flowers towards a large coach house in the back of the property. The night air was redolent with the scent of flowers and freshly-dewed grass. Julian took in a deep breath and almost felt dizzy from all the scents he was able to pick out. There were rose bushes to his left, an apple tree in the far corner, jasmine along the fence and a running brook that they passed over on a small footbridge. He forced his eyes open as he realized they had nearly closed and focused once more on Daemon. The trembling was still there.

Don't get me wrong. The way you handled things with William and all the others was really noble. Kingly. Julian struggled to find the words to describe how well Daemon had behaved. *I mean you could have just crushed all of them, but, not only did you defuse the issue with Heath and Selene, but you made what you said seem like a benediction. I know that Balthazar appreciated that.*

Daemon did not say anything again for a long moment. *I did it for you.*

Julian frowned. *You mean you agreed with my reasoning, right?*

Yes... and no. I did it because you asked me to. And, upon reflection, it was the right thing to do, Daemon admitted. *But I mostly did it because you wished for it and you would have been upset if I had not.*

Julian was the one to be stunned into silence this time. *That's a pretty big deal.*

You are my fledgling. You have more power over me than you know, that was said so softly that Julian almost didn't hear it.

I'll keep that in mind so I don't abuse it, Julian assured him and squeezed the hand that was trembling more than before. That squeeze steadied Daemon.

Arcius stepped up to a white painted door with a bronze knocker and handle. He turned to smile at them.

"This is the coach house where our Acolytes stay," Arcius explained. "You will be staying in the Blue Room. An Acolyte is already awaiting you there."

I will need more than one. I am assuming that they do not wish me to drain their Acolytes to death, Daemon said.

Yeah, that would be more than likely.

"Uh, Arcius, Daemon is hungrier than that," Julian found himself translating again as the Vampire King seemed not inclined to speak out loud any time soon.

Arcius was not in the least bit flustered. "I shall have more readied. How many would be sufficient."

A dozen, Daemon answered.

"Do you have *twelve* you can spare?" Julian asked, sensing just from the size of the house that a dozen would stretch House Ravenscroft to the limit considering these Acolytes had to feed the other members of the house, too, and recover.

Arcius froze for just a millisecond, but then answered smoothly, "I can call in some Acolytes that live off property to assist."

I will hunt tomorrow, but tonight we must remain here in seclusion, if possible, Daemon answered, clearly not pleased at his weakness.

"Do whatever you can," Julian said to Arcius.

The Confessor nodded and opened the door into the coach house. Julian's first impression was that it was a comfortable and luxurious spa retreat. There were a lot of candles and low light, dark wood and neutral wall colors. It was soothing.

Arcius led them to a second floor room to the right. Like its name, the room was done in shades of blue from the palest blue walls to a midnight blue comforter on a bed that could have hosted an orgy. The bed was in a separate room to their left. There looked to be a full ensuite bathroom in there as well.

The space before them probably would have been classified as a "sitting" room as there were couches, chairs, a fireplace and several small end tables, but it seemed far more like a high end lounge space to Julian. The reason was that the couches and chairs were overly large and deep, allowing two people to lie down on them easily. A young man dressed in tan silk pants only rose from one of those chairs. He bowed low. Julian's palms were suddenly sweaty.

"Jacob, these are our very special guests that I told you about,"

Arcius said with careful enunciation of every word. "King Daemon is recovering his strength after a long sleep and will need to feed from more than just you tonight. So he will be your only visitor. You will need to rest afterwards.."

"I understand, Master Arcius," Jacob spoke softly, still bowing.

Jacob was pretty. Blond curls framed an almost heart-shaped face. He had blue eyes and pink lips with teeth that were dazzling white. His bare chest showed sleek muscles under velvety golden skin. The silk pants did not hide the already considerable erection he had.

Julian's gaze flickered between Daemon and Jacob. Did Daemon find Jacob attractive? Did it matter considering he was going to feed from twelve different people that night?

The scent of sex and blood was heavy in the air in the coach house and Julian wondered if Daemon would have sex with any or all of his partners. Would Julian just watch if he did this? Did Julian want to participate? He felt territorial about Daemon, but he wasn't sure how much of these acts of feeding were about *him* versus just having a meal. How personal was it really?

He wiped his palms surreptitiously on the fronts of his pants, but he knew he looked tense. He *was* tense, but it was a *good* tense in a way. Excitement mixed with uncertainty. He felt this way every time he stepped into a mystery. Daemon was the ultimate mystery.

"All right. This room is yours for as long as you wish it. You may sleep here without worry as there are no windows if you do not wish to retire–"

"In Balthazar's room?" Julian grinned impishly which had Arcius chuckling.

"Yes, if you do not wish Balthazar's," Arcius agreed.

This will be fine, Daemon sounded hungry as he said this.

"We're totally good, Arcius. I think Daemon wants to… ah, *start,*" Julian explained.

Daemon was looking at the still bowing Jacob as if he were a glass of water in the desert. His red eyes were like living flames.

"I will leave you three, but will return with more Acolytes soon," Arcius told them. "Do you have any questions, King Daemon?"

Daemon had already shrugged off the beautiful fur coat and slung it over the back of one chair. *I have none.*

"We're all good." Julian nodded and gave a rather weak smile.

Arcius studied him for a moment, but then nodded and headed for the door. Before he did, he reached out and put one of those huge hands on Julian's right shoulder and gave it a comforting squeeze. Julian immediately calmed down a little.

It will be all right. This will become normal. You are safe.

All of these things were in that touch and Julian was grateful for it. It was only after Arcius passed out of the room and shut the door–so quietly for such a big man–that Julian noticed that Daemon was watching him like a hawk rather than regarding Jacob.

What's wrong? Julian asked.

I should be asking you this. You are not... not used to feeding. Of course, you are not. I did not consider this. Arcius did. Daemon's red eyes did not blink.

You can't be mad at Arcius about that! He was just being nice!

I am not angry with him–though he should ASK before he touches you–I was just realizing that we have much to learn about one another, Daemon admitted.

Julian might have clarified *who* Daemon thought Arcius should ask about touching him–Julian or Daemon–but he wanted the Vampire King to feed so he let it go.

We do. But that's part of the adventure, isn't it? We've stepped off this cliff together. Now we have to see where we end up.

Julian smiled in what he hoped was a comforting way, but it was really unnerving to have Jacob still just *bowing* there, all silent and erect.

Daemon surprised him by drawing his fingers down Julian's right cheek and letting them linger beneath his chin.

You are my ultimate adventure.

Then the Vampire King was turning from him to Jacob again. Julian's skin still burned from where Daemon had touched him. He stood there, though, rooted to the spot as Daemon stalked over to the young man.

Daemon's hands feathered through Jacob's curls and he pulled the Acolyte upright in a firm, but gentle grip so that Jacob was looking into his eyes. Jacob's pink lips parted and he let out a little gasp. He was staring up at Daemon as if he saw a *god*.

"Your eyes," Jacob whispered, "they're as red as blood."

And that was all he got to say, because Daemon tipped him back into almost a half swoon position and fastened his mouth against Jacob's throat. Julian watched as Daemon *swallowed* mouthful after mouthful of Jacob's *life*. The earthy scent of cum and the coppery smell of blood filled the room. Julian's fangs extended and he was salivating. But it wasn't for Jacob.

There was a *scent* rising up from Daemon that was so warm and welcoming and *needful*. Like fresh baked cookies on a cold day. Or the refreshing taste of icy cold beer when it was scalding hot out. Or that perfect spritz of cologne that meant male and beautiful and strong. His stomach suddenly felt like an empty sack and he was weak in the knees.

In seeming moments, Daemon was tenderly picking up the woozy Jacob and helping him to the couch to stare blankly out at the room. The front of his pants showed a wet stain. He had cum just from Daemon drinking from him. But that was all Julian saw of Jacob because the Vampire King fluidly turned towards him and all Julian could see was Daemon. All he wanted to see was Daemon.

Drink, my fledgling, my Julian, my jewel.

Daemon opened the veins in his own wrist again for Julian though there would have been no need as his fangs were razor sharp, but the Vampire King was taking care of him with this. Dark red blood traveled in trails down his arm. He offered his arm to Julian.

Julian grasped it and his tongue snuck out and licked up one long trail of coppery, sweet and salty blood. Daemon's other arm wrapped around his waist and Julian felt his own erection pressed against the Vampire King's. If he'd had any ability to think he would have measured the length of it with his hand, but he couldn't. He only knew that it felt like a bar against his fluttering stomach.

His lips finally fastened onto the wound directly on Daemon's wrist and he *sucked* long and hard. The hot liquid slid over his tongue and burned down his throat to then pool in his belly like a warm lake. Electric sparks went through his body like he'd touched a live socket.

He pressed his front up against Daemon's, hating his clothing with a passion. Why was he dressed?! Why hadn't he just come here nude? But he was too busy clinging to Daemon's wrist, feeling the light brushes of Daemon's lips on his temple and hair, to be capable of stripping himself.

But then he was being laid down on the couch and his clothing was being taken off by clever, strong hands. He was utterly bare. He felt the leather of the couch against his ass and back. That wrist–and the blood, the glorious blood–was gone. But then Daemon's lips were on his. Deep kisses that seemed to reach into the cold core of him and warm him.

Then Daemon was gone.

Julian rolled his head to the side, unable to move as the sparks ran through him, seeking Daemon's form. Jacob was already being carried out of the room by Arcius and a middle aged woman was being brought in. She wasn't beautiful in the traditional sense, but her smile had Julian smiling almost drunkenly back. Daemon was so gentle with her. Her eyelids fluttered closed in absolute pleasure as he drank from her, too.

And then Daemon was back with him again.

This time it wasn't his wrist he offered–which had already healed–but the skin over his right areola. He drew a sharp fingernail an inch across his skin and a red line appeared. Blood, dark as rubies ran like ribbons down his chest.. Daemon laid down on top of him, the leather pants and boots having disappeared at some point, too.

Julian swiped his tongue over the running red stuff, but he had some control to actually fasten his lips onto that tempting nipple, too. He rasped his teeth over it as he *sucked*. Daemon's body *jerked* above him. That cock–which Julian thought couldn't be less than eight inches–plumped further against their bellies.

Blood formed a "milk mustache" over the top of Julian's upper lip as he continued to nurse on Daemon's nipple and not the cut. He had to pull off to lick it away. Daemon helped him with light, cat-like swipes of his tongue over Julian's face. The Vampire King then urged him to the open cut and Julian drank again.

His own cock was actually tingling. He felt wetness between them and knew he was leaking precum. He actually wasn't sure if he hadn't already had his release once already, but he felt quite capable of cumming an infinite amount of times at that moment. He wrapped his legs around Daemon's waist and rubbed up against him frantically.

But no matter how hard he tried to hold onto the Vampire King, it seemed that Daemon was quite capable of escaping to feed them both. Julian found himself sprawled on the couch, covered by Daemon's fur coat to keep him warm even though the fire crackled and popped and gave off some lovely heat. Besides, he felt *on fire* with Daemon's blood running through his veins. Yet he wanted Daemon to warm him, but the Vampire King was across the room again.

He watched as Daemon drained a middle-aged man that he almost didn't recognize as Dr. Stone. The man was wearing his white lab coat as if he had just stepped out of the ER to provide sustenance for his Vampire masters. His gaze locked on Julian, but Julian couldn't focus on him. He was floating in a sea of ecstasy.

Then Daemon was with him fully again.

The Vampire King's naked body was, once more, on top of Julian's. Writhing and thrusting and grinding and giving. More blood. This time from his *throat*. Julian wrapped his arms around Daemon's neck. He feathered his fingers in the Vampire King's raven hair. The strands were so soft that he simply couldn't have been human.

Never been human.

In between feedings, Julian found himself looking up at the ceiling and no longer at where Daemon supped. What happened there was *not* important. It was only important when Daemon was with *him*. His gaze drifted up to the ceiling. At first, it was just a ceiling painted white. But then it seemed to him that the ceiling was made out of clouds and that those clouds parted to reveal a night black sky filled with alien stars and two moons: one red, one blue.

So beautiful, he murmured.

And he thought he heard his mother's voice say the same. *We've found something so amazing. I can't wait to share it with Julian...*

A long tear trailed down his left cheek as it felt like he was soaring.

Mom, Dad, I wish I could share this with YOU. You would have loved Daemon and Balthazar and Arcius. You would have been fascinated with them all, asking countless questions and recording every little detail. You would have chosen to become Vampires, if given the choice, so that you would have had more time to learn. But someone stole that from you. From me. From the world.

Daemon was with him again and offered his throat once more. The painful thoughts fluttered away. Their bodies seemingly became *one.* Julian's balls drew tight against his body. His cock *thrummed.* He pushed up helplessly against that larger, muscled body, seeking release even as so much blood flowed into his mouth that a little dribbled out of his lips and down his chin. Daemon grasped both globes of his ass and pulled him impossibly close. They rubbed furiously against one another. Cocks sliding past one another. Heat building like the magma in a volcano about to blow.

Julian pulled off Daemon's throat and their lips were on each other's. They kissed and kissed and kissed. He should have needed air. If he had been *mortal* he would have. But not now. Now he was so much more. Daemon had made him so much more. Their tongues entwined even as Julian's cock shuddered. He tightened his grip on Daemon. He would not let him go.

Stay with me. Stay with me. Stay with me, he begged.

Forever, Daemon answered.

And Julian was cumming. That hot release was like death, but also made him feel the most alive. His seed spilled all over Daemon's skin. All over his own skin. They rode out the spasms of twin pleasure. His lips melded against Daemon's and they kissed until his head fell back and he let out a cry of total completion. He went limp. All energy gone. Satiated with blood and sex and Daemon.

Daemon laid them both down onto the couch fully, cradling Julian alongside him. Julian just breathed, incapable of doing anything else, as he saw both Daemon and the Ever Dark night sky above them. Daemon pressed lazy kisses against his temples.

Then Julian felt them *lift* into the air.

They moved up past where the ceiling should have been and they were in the air. He could still feel them on the couch with Daemon's fur coat over them, their sweat and cum-slicked bodies intertwined, but they were also up in the sky.

Flying.

They were ravens. Flying together over Nightvallen. The impossible beauty of that city of pale stone flowed beneath their wings as they glided on warm breezes. Side by side. Into the night.

Julian fell asleep in the Vampire King's arms, but in his dreams, they were still flying in Ever Dark. In the freedom and beauty of the world where no sun ever shone.

FAITH

⚜

Earlier...

Vampire Confessor Fiona Darksilver stood in the center of the Siryn Blood Den. Her silver eyes scanned the Vampires who darted curious and some angry glances at her. It was never good when a Confessor of her level came into a Blood Den. They all knew that.

Vampire Confessors Donato and Sloan had been called to this address, because Julian Harrow had been spotted here. Yet now everyone claimed it had been a false alarm. Even her fellow Confessors were saying so. But there was a *vagueness* in their recollections of the evening and the recording of who entered and exited had apparently become corrupted rather conveniently.

I smell Eyros' interference, she thought and narrowed her eyes as she scanned those all present again.

None met her gaze this time. They all sensed her anger and didn't want her to take it out on them. A Confessor could sanction any Vampire, which could mean imprisonment or worse. In this case, it would be the "or worse".

Caemorn had made it quite clear that anyone who stood against them was to be eliminated. Even though these Vampires appeared to truly know *nothing*–at least not anymore–might not matter to him. If she reported what happened here, he would require them to be executed. She didn't want that. But she had to somehow salvage the evening or Caemorn would focus on the failures here.

She snapped her fingers at Donato and Sloan, indicating that they should follow her into one of the private rooms. She chose the first one on her right. When she stepped inside there was a particular perfume she recognized.

"Sophia Strange," she said out loud and her stomach fell.

A Seeyr was involved in this. A very powerful Seeyr. Sophia had long been suspected of treachery, but there had never been any proof of it. She always danced just out of the Order's grasp. Caemorn though would see her presence here as proof of guilt. But Sophia was a beloved Seeyr and had many allies. Harming her would harm the Order. But Caemorn wouldn't see it that way. He would only see betrayal.

Donato blinked almost sleepily at her–more proof of mind control and brainwashing–and said, "What, my lady?"

She turned around to face him, her cloak snapping behind her like a living thing. The beads in her hair clicked. "Sophia Strange was here. She was in this room."

Sloan frowned. Her forehead puckered. "I don't–"

"You don't *remember*? Is that what you were going to say? Because you don't remember Julian Harrow being here either, but I'm certain he was." Fiona couldn't help the sharpness in her tone.

It had Sloan flinching as if she had been struck.

"I'm trying my best, my lady, to give you the information you want. But I cannot lie to you and tell you what I did not experience," she whined. "I simply do not recall Sophia Strange being in the Blood Den. We allowed no one to leave after getting the message about the Harrow boy."

"And yet she *was* here and not all that long ago. This evening definitely. Yet somehow she is gone and somehow no one remembers her." Fiona took in a second deep breath of the air. There was another scent. Something not familiar and yet it tantalized her nostrils. She felt she should know it. It smelled primal to her somehow. Was it the Harrow boy? "And someone was here with her. But I'm betting you don't remember him either. Don't answer that. I already know what you will say."

The other Confessors said nothing, but they did glance at one another. What was there to say? She was claiming they were either incompetent or brainwashed. Either was unacceptable for a Confessor. Confessors were to be strong enough of mind to resist an Eyros attack, but they had not.

The whole Blood Den is brainwashed though, she thought with a touch of alarm. *It would take dozens of Eyros days to accomplish this, but it has been done in less than one night! And somehow I do not think a troop of Eyros came in here.*

That left two possibilities. The first was that the Vampire King himself had come to spirit away Sophia Strange and Julian Harrow. But, even if such a being truly did exist, why would he come to get those two?

And the message that had been received by the Order was that Julian had come in alone. She supposed if the Vampire King did exist then he could make himself invisible, but why would he? And why would he bring Julian to a Siryn Blood Den then erase everyone's memories of them being there? That simply made no sense. The other possibility was more likely and, in a way, far more worrisome.

Balthazar Ravenscroft, she named that second possibility in her head.

Even though Balthazar was young, he had managed to overthrow and kill Roan Tithe, his own Master. Roan had been brilliant at mind control especially over his fledglings. But Balthazar had ended him with extreme prejudice.

And Arcius came to his side. Convinced the Council to simply exile instead of execute him as the law requires, she thought with some bitterness.

It wasn't that she believed that what Roan had been doing was right. No, absolutely not. It should have been dealt with by the Council or the Order long before Balthazar killed him. But Roan was a veteran of the War of the Immortals. Excuses were made for him. Lenience was offered. He had sacrificed part of his soul and mind for all of them. This had granted him centuries to abuse his fledglings while everyone turned a blind eye.

She wasn't even angry that Arcius had argued vociferously on Balthazar's behalf. He'd made the point that if they had intervened when they should have the murder would never have happened. But few wanted to take on the responsibility of failing a whole House.

Interfering in a House was something that was simply never to be done if one could help it. Also, people knew that Balthazar was one of Arcius' projects after all. One of those broken, brilliant and beautiful young men that attracted the Vampire Confessor's love, devotion and desire to bring back into the fold. So they had dismissed many of his arguments.

All of Arcius' points she had understood. It was the fact that Arcius had abandoned *her* for Balthazar that still smarted. She had been his apprentice for well over 200-years, but he had thrown her over for a Vampire he'd known only half a century. A Vampire that had killed his Master. A Vampire that did not even *believe*. Yet Arcius hadn't even hesitated when the Council had told him that the only way they would consider not executing Balthazar for the unforgivable sin of killing his Master–even if it was to save himself and the other members of House Tithe–was if Arcius went into exile himself.

"I accept. I will go into exile," Arcius had said without a moment's thought to the Council that had loomed above him on the half-moon dais.

Fiona had been standing beside her and she couldn't help her gasp. She'd turned to him, her hands clenched before her chest and said, "But you can't! You can't leave!"

He'd touched her hands gently with one of his large bear-like paws and smiled down at her beatifically. "But I must. We failed to protect them. We did not rein in Roan when we had the chance and now look what has happened."

"But it doesn't have to be *you* who goes! It's not your fault! You wanted to do something, but others wouldn't–."

He pressed two fingers to her lips to stop her from mentioning Caemorn's name and bringing upon herself censure at best and exile at worst. Caemorn had been the one to nix most of Arcius' arguments. He had taken pleasure in doing it, too.

"I am a member of the Order. I am responsible as much as any other," he told her.

"You are a member of the Order no longer, Arcius Kane. You are hereby exiled with the rest of House Tithe," Councillor Thalen said and rapped his gavel on the wooden table.

"No, no! That's impossible–"

"Fiona." Arcius gently held her.

He was still smiling. His eyes were filled with tears, but *not* at leaving the Ever Dark or losing his position or anything like that. He felt *her* pain, but he was still going to leave her despite the fact that she was in agony because of it.

She'd known even then–beyond her own pain–that the loss of Arcius was more than unjust, it would be a detriment to the Order. He was not simply a Senior Confessor with a bright heart and brilliant mind, but also a balance to those in the Order–like Caemorn–who put politics first instead of faith.

Arcius was a figure whom other Confessors rallied around. He was someone who could have blunted Caemorn's more authoritarian and detrimental policies over the years. For if Arcius opposed something, there would at least be a debate. He had been an incredibly powerful figure though he himself had never seemed to grasp that. There were rumors that the Order had been considering replacing Caemorn with Arcius at some point. That was until he was exiled.

"My lady," Donato said hesitantly, noticing her lack of focus.

She snapped back to the present and zeroed in on him. "What?"

"What would you have us do?" he asked.

"Balthazar Ravenscroft," she said the name of the man who had stolen Arcius not only from her, but from the Order itself and allowed Caemorn to run wild. "I believe he is behind this. He and his House."

Sloan was frowning again. Fiona was really starting to hate that frown. "But, if I recall rightly, Balthazar has no love for the Immortals or the Order. He does not believe in anything. So why would he help the Harrow boy or this – this potential rogue Immortal?"

Fiona repressed a sigh. Sloan did not understand Balthazar's psychology. He'd been damaged by people in authority so he pushed back and even denied their existence. He would be one to help Daemon, not to help the Vampire King because of his rank, but to simply thumb his nose at the Order and the Council that had thrust him out.

But Arcius would believe. He has always believed that Daemon was out there. Sleeping and waiting to return. He would urge Balthazar to take his side as well.

Her heart clenched at the thought of Arcius being on the opposite side of the Order. The opposite side of *her*. Even if Daemon was real and the First Among Equals, the Vampires could never allow him to rule them. The Immortals were rather like the Greek and Roman gods in her opinion. Powerful, but full of vices and not fit to rule justly or wisely. The way things were now was better.

But a small voice in her head whispered, *And what of Caemorn? Do you think he is just and wise? Do you think he is worthy of leadership? No, you do not. Arcius should be Preceptor. But instead he was sent away and now he might be on the opposite side of you in this battle.*

"We are going to watch House Ravenscroft," she finally informed the two other Confessors. "And once we have the proof we need we will go in."

She desperately wanted to speak to Arcius first, but the moment he saw her, House Ravenscroft would hide whatever it was doing. If the House was giving King Daemon sanctuary, she would lose whatever chance she had of stopping his return. He would be weak now, just having awakened. Later it might be too late if even a tenth of the stories about his powers were true.

"Tell no one of what we are doing. The two of you are to go dark," she informed them. "What we do now is crucial to the very heart of the Vampire world."

Both bowed low.

* * *

"Is the yelling over?" Sophia Strange asked as she peeked into the room. She had changed into a yellow baby doll dress with strappy sandals that somehow made her look younger to Balthazar than before. She caught sight of William and came over, "Oh, William, don't cry." She crouched down by him and patted his back. "It's over now. Balthazar won't be angry with you forever."

"You see that in the future, do you?" Balthazar asked archly.

She smiled up at him. "You're even feeling bad about it now. Though you shouldn't." She went back to addressing William who looked at her with a tear streaked face. "You were very wrong, William, to be so disrespectful to our king and his fledgling. I know you won't do it again and will be a loyal subject, but you must understand how very wrong you were."

"I won't ever do it again!" William sobbed.

Balthazar did feel badly. Even though William and the others had earned his shouting and, if he were a different sort of Master, he would have done far more than that. But still, he hated to see his people upset. He knew he was indulgent and that was why their seeming betrayal had hurt so much more. Even now, they all clustered around the edges of the room like shamed children. He pinched the top of his nose. He felt a hand on his back. He opened his eyes, but he already knew it was Christian touching him.

Comforting me.

He looked into his fledgling's beautiful face. He found himself focusing on those lips especially. Christian had kissed him. He was pretty sure that it was because the young man had lost himself in the joy of feeding and wasn't truly personal. But still. It was a start. And now Christian was touching him to comfort him. That hand immediately left his back as if Christian sensed what he was thinking.

"Thank you for keeping your temper," Christian said quietly. "It would be a terrible tragedy to make Julian and my introduction to your House accompanied by another death."

"You are too kind, Christian, considering William there—though he looks like a choirboy is old enough to be your grandfather and is not at all sweet—would have ripped your best friend's heart out if he could," Balthazar remarked dryly.

Christian's head tipped up. "There was no chance of that happening."

"We don't know that," Balthazar protested.

"On the contrary, Daemon entered your room as a pack of wolves," Christian replied. "I am pretty sure he could take on one Vampire all by himself. In fact, I am pretty sure he can take on all of us at the same time."

"He appeared in your quarters as a pack of wolves, my lord?" Isabel asked. Her right hand fluttered by her string of pearls.

"He did," Christian assured her.

"Oh, yes, it was quite *dramatic*. He likes to be dramatic. I mean he levitated William." Balthazar bit down on the laugh he wanted to let out. That was impressive and funny at the same time. Or would have been if it had not been caused by William's absolute foolishness.

I should have called a House meeting. I should have explained everything, but I didn't. I let rumors swirl and didn't let them voice their fears. This is somewhat my fault, he realized. *I was the foolish one, but I was so put off my game by having Christian and Julian finally here that I didn't think.*

"Bloodline Weryn," Isabel whispered and she twisted her strand of beads so hard that it snapped and the pearl scattered everywhere.

"Oh, damn," Balthazar muttered and went to lean down to collect some of them.

But Isabel grasped the front of his shirt and her eyes were frantic. "He really is our king, isn't he? The First Among Equals? And we—we *attacked* him!"

Balthazar wanted to say that if she desired someone to confirm that Daemon was the Vampire King she should seek out Arcius. He didn't believe it. Except that wasn't quite true any longer. He'd seen some of what Daemon could do—and though the man was really weak right now—his powers were *incredible*. Further, he had all the powers that the Vampire King was supposed to have.

They hadn't seen Armageddon yet, but no Vampire he knew could perform two of the Bloodlines' powers, let alone the half dozen he'd already displayed. Further, he came from Nightvallen. Also, Julian bore his mark. And, perhaps most importantly, the Order was trying to hush it all up. His eyes met Christian's. He knew that this very scientifically minded fledgling of his had already accepted that Daemon was king based upon facts. So why was he so resistant to it?

He found himself saying, "Yes, he is, but he didn't seem to mind that our people attacked him. He actually praised me and all of you. Didn't you notice?"

She blinked at him. He frowned. He sounded like a little boy who had been given a pat on the head. He didn't need anyone's approval, let alone this supposed *king*. He would only call a person "king" or "majesty" or "Master" if they had earned his respect. Daemon had yet to do that. He'd acted magnanimously with William to be sure. But that was hardly enough to win over Balthazar.

"Just because he might be the Daemon of legend doesn't really mean anything, Isabel. We threw off the yoke of the other Immortals when they used us as cannon fodder. If he thinks he can just come in and rule us all he's got another thing coming," he told her.

Isabel though was looking off into the distance, eyes filled with a mixture of shock and awe. Her hands loosened on his shirt front and she drifted over to William's side. Sophia was still trying to coax him up, but William wanted to remain kneeling until Balthazar allowed him to rise. Another stab of guilt went through Balthazar. He glanced over at Christian. His fledgling was regarding William out of sympathetic eyes. That was enough to move him.

"Enough of this," Balthazar muttered. He leaned down and picked up William into his arms. The Vampire weighed practically nothing and looked up at him out of huge eyes in a tearstained face. "You really are *adorable*. Dangerously so, William. I am still very angry with you. You know that, don't you?"

"Yes, my lord," he sniffled and lowered his head. Fat tears slid down his face and landed on Balthazar's shirt. "Oh, no!" He tried desperately to blot them, knowing how particular Balthazar was about his clothing. "I'm so sorry!"

"Enough with the apologies. I know you are," Balthazar said. "Christian, we're going to take William to his room then we are going to finish what we started in the coach house." Christian nodded. He then addressed the room, "The rest of you go back to your evening. I'm sure there will be a lot of gossiping, but save your questions until tomorrow. We will be having a House meeting where I will try to answer them all. But know this." His voice grew very stern, "Daemon and Julian are our guests. I want there to be no misunderstandings about that. I do not care what other feelings you might have about them. They are to be treated with respect."

There were nods all around and the Vampires drifted away in groups. They were already chattering softly amongst themselves. He was sure that the House hadn't had this kind of excitement in *years*.

Before Isabel left, she looked back at him and he couldn't completely read her expression at first. She had been very devout back when Roan had ruled their House. Her faith had waned after they had been exiled though she still prayed with Arcius weekly. He'd assumed her faith to be something to hang onto when Roan was vile. Now, he saw a feverous light in her eyes again.

He wondered what those that did believe in the old tales about Daemon being their savior would think about the fact that he was their guest. The exiled House hosted the Vampire King. Maybe Arcius was right that this truly could be their ticket back into the Vampire world.

Sophia spoke up, "Before you go, there's something you need to know, Balthazar."

"What is it? Do you need another piece of furniture? I don't mind the COD thing. Quite convenient really," he teased her.

As he said this, William rested his head tentatively on Balthazar's shoulder. William always loved to be cuddled. It was something that Roan had enjoyed withholding from him. He let William snuggle down. He worried for a moment that Christian might be jealous, but one glance at his Spock-like fledgling and the thought fled. Christian was not worried about his place with him. Balthazar nearly shone with joy at that.

"Oh, good! But no more things are arriving tonight. At the end of the week though I am expecting some *exquisite* linen," she informed him, practically swooning at the thought of sheets. "You're so generous with me, Lord Balthazar."

He grunted. "Of course. I'm expecting to hear about that greatness you promised me in return at some point."

She giggled. "You're so funny! But really one of my predictions has already come through so you mustn't be *greedy*."

"What prediction?" Christian asked.

Balthazar winced. He knew which one it was. She had said that Daemon was going to be the exact person he was looking for. And in that one instant when Daemon had praised him, he had felt *something*. And Daemon sparing William after dealing with the mutiny so well had also been rather a relief. It was as if he had someone he could turn to even steadier than Arcius.

Daemon had that quality of command. But he shook himself. He was reading too much into this. That needy part inside of him that still wanted a Master on some level–since Roan had been such a monster and not up the task–had latched onto a commanding voice and demeanor. That was all. It didn't mean anything about Daemon was worthy or that he needed him.

Sophia just smiled enigmatically, not answering Christian, before saying, "And one other thing."

"What?" he asked with a sense of dread. She'd already told him about the linen. He supposed dresses or something were next.

But that wasn't what she had to tell him. "I'm afraid that you'll have to go *out* to eat this evening. Daemon will have drained all the Acolytes."

"All of them?" he asked faintly.

"Well, over a dozen," she qualified. "So you see there simply won't be enough to go around. And since you're the type of Vampire Lord that feeds himself *last*…"

He groaned and tipped his head back.

"I won't feed, my lord," William offered. "I know you have to feed for two."

"William, you look like you need to recover at home. And, besides, going out would be good," Christian put in. "Balthazar, you can show me how to hunt and use mind control. I wish to start my education as soon as possible."

"But ... but ..." Balthazar pathetically bleated. "We need to be *alone* and –"

"We will be alone. Well, us and a city full of people," Christian said with a shrug. "Besides, there is nothing really that interests me in the coach house."

Other than the kissing and touching and beds! Nothing there of interest at all.

But he already knew that Christian wasn't going to sleep with him that night. He was also pretty sure there would be no repeat of the kissing or touching. So maybe it was best if they were out and about. Christian loved to learn. He loved to teach. That could be the start of a relationship between them.

Balthazar grinned. "All right, I will take you out hunting then."

KINDS

Hunting.

That word was not something that Christian usually associated with obtaining a meal. One went to the grocery store or out to a restaurant or even just to the refrigerator. But hunting? To hunt? To have to go out and actually hunt down food? Not to mention that the food would be as smart as you were? And for it to be quite illegal to eat? In fact, to be found out was to threaten all Vampire-kind.

Nothing to be nervous about, Christian thought dryly.

His face reflected back at him in the mirror though and it showed he *was* nervous. His lips were pressed tightly together. His jaw clenched and unclenched. His fangs though were not coming out. It was as if eating was the last thing he wanted to do.

Because we're going to be eating from people. But not killing them. And Balthazar will be the one feeding from them and me from him.

He smoothed his hands down the front of his shirt and took in a breath to steady himself. His reflection–*guess that was a myth about Vampires not being able to see themselves in the mirror*–looked slightly more at ease. As he usually did when he was anxious about something, he listed out all the reasons that things would be fine.

Balthazar knows what he's doing. He may be slightly ridiculous when it comes to certain things. A little reactive. Very emotional. But he was able to stop that entire room of Vampires with the force of his mind. Humans should be even easier to control. So... I'm safe with him.

Yet this wouldn't be an easy encounter with an Acolyte who wished to be with them, who wanted it. These people would not be willing.They might even be afraid. When they realized that Balthazar was a Vampire, what would they do? Or would they simply already be in a trance?

He was certain that Julian was already deep into the business of feeding from Daemon. His best friend was always eager to try new things. Julian would leap before he looked all the time. There would be the crash later when he came down from eating strange food, drinking unclean water, rappelling off that ledge, but while Julian was in the moment, he would be golden. Christian was not that way. He studied everything from every angle and, truthfully, was not a big fan of change.

And becoming a Vampire is the biggest change of all.

"Christian? Everything okay?" Balthazar asked from his bedroom.

Christian had left the Vampire Lord fussing around with the bed since it was now clear that Daemon and Julian would not be using his bedroom again. Christian saw his actions rather like a cat inspecting where it normally slept after another cat had sat there.

"I'm fine," Christian said with a final look at himself in the mirror. "Ready to go."

Christian stepped out of the bathroom and saw that the bed had been completely stripped and remade for the second time that night. Christian's eyebrows rose.

"Didn't you already change the linen after Julian threw up? Are you changing it *again*, because Daemon laid there for like *one* hour?" Christian asked.

Both of them looked over at the perfectly made bed that was heaped with mounds of pillows, a dark purple comforter and a fur blanket lying across the bottom of the bed.

"Well, I was having your room prepared with fresh linen so I thought I would do my own at the same time." Balthazar shrugged.

"*My* room?" Christian couldn't keep the shock out of his voice.

He couldn't have heard this right. Wasn't *this* his room? Or rather, the room he shared with Balthazar? He had been wondering what the sleeping arrangements were going to be. He had been planning on erecting a pillow barrier between them at the very least. Yet here Balthazar was offering him a room of his own.

"Yes, would you like to see it before we leave? Can't take too long as the night is getting away from us," Balthazar told him casually.

Too casually. He knows this is a big deal.

"I thought..." Christian stopped. He wasn't sure how to phrase this, but then decided direct was best. "I thought you intended for me to have to sleep in here with you."

Balthazar cleared his throat and shuffled a little bit, which was incongruent to his elegant attire and demeanor. "I did, but then I realized that's not what *you* wanted. Besides, everyone needs their own space."

"Where is it? My room, that is." Christian wasn't sure he believed that this room existed.

"Two doors down." Balthazar tipped his head in the direction of Christian's room.

"Not right next door? No adjoining chambers or anything like that?" Christian fully expected there to be some way other than the hallway door for Balthazar to get to him.

But the Vampire Lord shook his head. "Like I said: everyone needs their own space. Shall we go see it?" He offered again.

Christian though had not moved. He felt like he was waiting for the other shoe to drop. There *had* to be some catch. This was Balthazar after all. The Vampire Lord sighed and rubbed his forehead.

"I can see what you're thinking, Christian, even though I can't quite read your mind," Balthazar said. "And you think that there's some funny business going on here."

"Quite frankly, *yes*." Christian crossed his arms over his chest. "You've made it quite clear about what you think a relationship

between a Master and Fledgling must be. And it involves lots of...
touching. And definitely sleeping in the same room."

Balthazar flashed one of those grins that Christian was finding less
annoying and almost endearing. "You are right and wrong."

"Explain, please."

"That I *want* there to be touching and being together," Balthazar
gestured to the bed. "But not that there *must* be. I want you to want
me. It's as simple as that. And I can't make you do that."

Christian's arms unfolded and hung down by his sides. "After
everything I've seen you do, I'm pretty sure you *could* make me."

"I would *never* make you," Balthazar said and all of his usual
amusement was completely gone.

"No, of course, you wouldn't. Not after what Roan did to all of
you." Christian suddenly felt cold and rubbed his arms.

Balthazar obviously didn't want either of them to think about
Roan too long so he waggled his eyebrows as he said, "I notice that
you're also saying that I'm impressive? And powerful? And–"

"I think you're fully aware of your own power," Christian replied
dryly.

"But to hear it from one's fledgling is–how shall I say–wonderful?
Especially, if that fledgling is you," Balthazar answered. "Because you
don't exaggerate things."

"Hmmm, well, I think I have stroked your ego enough tonight."

Especially after that kiss. I don't know why I did that. Likely, the inti-
macy of the moment, but that should have had me withdrawing not moving
towards him like that.

"Then let's see your room and we shall be off."

Christian followed Balthazar out of the bedroom and two doors
down the hall. The Vampire Lord pushed open the door with his
fingertips and stepped back so that Christian could walk in first. He
moved inside, not sure what he expected.

The room was modern with clean lines, maple flooring and furniture with cool gray-blue walls. There was a king-sized bed with
neutral bedding. It looked cool and crisp. There was a desk with a
sleek Mac laptop. There was a walk-in closet that smelled pleasantly

of cedar. Finally, there was an en suite bathroom in icy white with dual pedestal sinks and a floor to ceiling glass-enclosed shower with multiple shower heads.

Christian padded out of the bathroom to where Balthazar was standing, waiting for him. While this was different from his room at Wingate–Wingate was more traditional with honey woods and country accents–but this room *felt* like him. It would make being here, away from his true home, easier.

"Well? How do you like it? You can, of course, change whatever you like. As Sophia has demonstrated, we have a substantial decorating budget," Balthazar said, rocking back and forth on his heels.

"It's fine as is. I think I'll let Sophia have my decorating budget," Christian said and he almost felt shy about it. "Thank you for this, Balthazar."

"Of course. I want you to feel this is your home, Christian," Balthazar said with a faint smile.

"I know you want that," Christian said.

He didn't say that *he* wanted that, too. All of this was too confusing. He was out of his usual spot and still wanted his life to go back to what it was. But that wasn't going to happen. His logical brain told him that he had to figure out how to go forward and not mourn for what was lost.

"Come, Christian, we only have a few hours before we must return." Balthazar extended a hand to him, gesturing Christian to proceed him out of the room.

Balthazar took them to the garage again like he had when they went to rescue Julian from the Siryn Blood Den, but this time instead of getting into one of the SUVs, the Vampire Lord took them to a jet black Mercedes convertible. Even though the air was chilly, Balthazar put down the top.

"You'll find that you don't feel the cold like you used to," Balthazar explained before he pulled the sedan out in a fluid, confident movement.

They were soon off the manor's grounds and onto the curving, darkened streets of the town. Balthazar did not head into the downtown where the Blood Den was, but instead got onto the highway that lead to the nearest large city about twenty minutes away.

The cold breeze was like a caress against Christian's skin. He leaned his head back against the headrest and closed his eyes as the luxury car raced over the asphalt like it was a spool of unending silk. He only opened them when Balthazar asked him a question.

"What did you say?" Christian asked. His mind had been obsessed with the whistle of the wind and he hadn't heard the question.

Balthazar gave him a wicked smile. "I asked what kind of prey did you want to hunt tonight."

"What *kind?*" Christian frowned.

Thad had Balthazar chuckling. He shifted gears and effortlessly moved around two semis and several speeding sedans. His move-ments were incredibly *precise.* Christian realized that Vampire reflexes were at least twice as fast as human ones, probably more than that. Balthazar hardly seemed to pay attention to the vehicles around them as he effortlessly weaved around them and left them in his dust. But there was never a sense that he didn't know the obstacles that were around them. Balthazar was *perfectly* aware of their surround-ings at all times.

The ultimate predator.

"Ah, I'm not suggesting different *species.* Obviously, humans are the best. Other animals will drive us crazy. So! The issue is what kind of human we go after," Balthazar explained.

"What kind of humans are there?" Christian frowned, his forehead puckering.

"Oh, Christian, for such a scientific mind you are being very unimaginative. Is that because you're worried about choosing anyone at all?" Balthazar fully turned his head towards Christian.

The urge to tell him to look at the road was high, especially when a car darted in front of them, but—without looking forward at all—Balthazar neatly avoided that maneuver and managed to snake through all of the traffic and into an empty span of road with no one by them.

Christian let out a breath that he turned into a sigh as if put upon.

"You tell me what you mean about different kinds. I don't lump humans together like you do."

"*Yet.* You'll start to see humanity differently after a time. You will have to. Otherwise, it will cause you too much distress," the last was said softly.

"We're not going to kill anyone, right?" Christian asked sharply. He thought he already knew the answer, but he wanted to be sure.

"Of course not." Balthazar reached to touch his shoulder, but instead lowered his hand quickly before he touched Christian.

Christian actually ached when Balthazar didn't touch him. He didn't dismiss this reaction immediately. He studied it. He realized—with a little start of discomfort as Balthazar was *still* an unknown quantity—that he was beginning to depend on the Vampire Lord to make him feel comfortable in this brand new world.

"I'm really dividing humanity into those we might find attractive—and that doesn't just mean physical attraction—and those... well, the *bad* ones. The *villains.* The ones that intend to do harm," Balthazar explained.

Christian thought about this. What Balthazar was asking him was whether he wanted to go after people that attracted him in some way or to stop those that were hurting others. He immediately had an answer.

"The bad ones," Christian said. "If we're going to hunt people let's at least pair it with doing something *good.*"

Balthazar merely nodded. He didn't question Christian's choice. In fact, Christian was pretty sure that Balthazar understood exactly why he wanted to go after those causing harm.

"How will we find the wrong doers though?" Christian asked as they silkily threaded their way through traffic and aimed for an exit that would take them through a very bad part of the nearby city.

"I can smell violence," Balthazar explained. His lips pursed as though that did not fully explain what he experienced. "The Eyros power of mind control is often seen as imposing one's will *upon* another. But that's not accurate. We see inside their minds and know exactly how to influence them."

"So you read their minds?" Christian qualified.

He gave a brief nod. "It's more and less than that. For example, I know that in that apartment building on the fourth floor, a man is about to rape a woman. Brutally. He intends to use a *hammer*."

Christian jerked back in his seat then said, "Let's stop that."

"All right." Again, there was no hesitation as Balthazar exited the highway and glided silently through the worn streets where the concrete was broken, the buildings were sad, and the people were afraid.

Balthazar turned their headlights off as soon as they left the highway. Christian immediately realized that he had no trouble seeing in the dark. In a way, the headlights had been a distraction. The Vampire Lord turned into an alleyway where the fire escapes surrounded them on both sides like an Escher painting. The purr of the engine was cut off as Balthazar pressed the engine button. Silence fell.

Except it wasn't really silent.

If Christian had still been human, the alleyway would have seemed quiet, but to his Vampiric senses it was anything but. There was a man on the first floor with sleep apnea. Christian could hear the labored breathing, followed by the ominous pause, and then a gasp as the man drank air down greedily. There was a woman on the second floor who had bad gas that night. She would fart and then let out a sigh of relief. There was a child on the third floor that was having nightmares and letting out little whimpers as if she were being chased. And then there was the couple on the fourth floor.

Even as a human he would have heard the sharp words between them. Hers were shrill with anger and fear. His were barks of rage that were barely contained. The hair on the back of Christian's neck stood on end. Violence was definitely in the air.

Balthazar got out of the car in one liquid movement. He didn't bother with putting the top up or even slipping the key fob that allowed the car to be turned on into his pocket. He simply left the key there and the car open. Christian was betting that no one stole from a Vampire and got away with it for very long. Besides, the night was long and deep. There was no one around in this stinking alleyway in this bad part of the city. They were the top predators in any event. Christian joined him.

"How do we get up?" Christian doubted that they were heading in the front door.

He was right. Balthazar crouched down and then lightly leaped up onto the first floor's fire escape. The metal did not even rattle when the Vampire Lord landed. Balthazar was about to release the ladder for him, but Christian made a movement to indicate he shouldn't. Christian was going to try to leap just as Balthazar had. The Vampire Lord grinned and stepped back from the railing so that Christian had plenty of room to land.

Christian felt rather like a cat as he crouched down and waggled his butt, winding up for the leap. And he did leap. He went up into the air but soared *past* the first stairwell, but not quite to the second. He started to fall back down. His hands scrabbled at the air. Balthazar caught him around the wrists and effortlessly hauled him up onto the fire escape. Christian's heart was pounding and he clutched at the Vampire Lord for long moments. Balthazar gently stroked his back, but was careful not to go lower. Christian had closed his eyes at some point and realized he was trembling.

"You did well," Balthazar assured him.

"I need to test my abilities in a controlled setting," Christian said, trying to keep any shaking out of his voice.

"I am here, Christian. I wouldn't let you do anything dangerous that I couldn't save you from. Now, let's go up. Quiet as mice," Balthazar said.

The Vampire Lord had let him go—his trembling had eased—and yet, Christian felt so *bereft*. Yet he knew that he was safe. Though this situation would have been dangerous to others, he knew that with Balthazar that it was controlled. He wasn't going to let his guard down, but he realized that he didn't need to be terrified either.

Christian was reminded of his and Julian's childhoods where they would play Bloody Mary or Ghosts in the Graveyard where they and their friends would be scared of the dark, but knew in the backs of their heads that they were truly safe in the upper middle class neighborhood. It was the same now. They were doing what seemed like a dangerous thing–what likely *was* a dangerous thing for others–but not for them. Balthazar was completely in control.

They ghosted up the black painted metal stairs. The metal didn't even rattle beneath their feet. Christian realized that he could consciously adjust the weight of his footsteps to make them utterly silent. It was *fascinating*. All too soon, they were crouched outside of the fourth story apartment where the couple was arguing. The woman's voice was soft and pleading. She was crying. Christian could hear the pain in her voice–the boyfriend had likely struck her–and was edging to get inside and end this.

But Balthazar held a hand on his shoulder and kept them crouching down just beneath the lip of the sill. Christian glanced over the top of it and was nearly blinded by two lamps on the side tables though they were low wattage. He blinked and his eyes teared. In that brief moment before being nearly blinded, he had seen a man–white, about six foot with tattoos all down his arms of skulls and vines, in a white t-shirt and faded jeans–gripping the shoulders of a dark-haired young woman with golden toned skin and green eyes. She wore jeans and a yellow top. Her makeup was streaked from tears and she was trying to twist out of the man's hands.

"I didn't!" she wailed. "I just went to *work*! Jason is my boss! I have to talk to him!"

The man shook her violently as if she was some kind of ragdoll. Her head snapped back and forth with a painful *clicking* sound. The apartment smelled of old blood, rancid food and despair. Christian knew that no one here was happy. The sense of being trapped was in every gray, dirty angle of the apartment. He couldn't stand it.

"I know you were flirting with him! I know what you are! You *whore*!" he snarled.

Christian's jaw tightened. He wanted to leap up and grasp this asshole by the throat and shake *him* until he knew what pain she felt. Before he knew it, he actually had leaped into the apartment. Balthazar hadn't stopped him.

The boyfriend caught sight of him and shouted, "Who the fuck are you?"

At first, Christian looked back at Balthazar who was leisurely coming in through the window. The Vampire Lord was letting him take the lead. Christian whipped around towards the couple as he heard the boyfriend throw the girl into the wall and advance upon him. She bounced off the plaster painfully and rubbed the back of her head with a dazed expression on her face. The boyfriend's lips were peeled back from his teeth in a snarl and his hands were raised up to punch Christian.

"Now, Christian, your reflexes are quite a bit better than his. Let him come at you so you can see what I mean practically," Balthazar said matter of factly.

Christian turned back to the boyfriend just as the bastard was throwing his first punch. Time seemed to slow to a crawl while Christian's movements appeared at normal speed. He effortlessly stepped outside of the punch's range. Another punch came and another. Again, simply stepping right or left kept him well out of getting hit.

"What the Hell?" the boyfriend shouted. The faintest trace of fear was entering his voice. Christian knew that his movements were inexplicably fast.

"Now, Christian, can you feel his mind? It's a coarse, pathetic thing–hardly used–but it's there. He's all spittal and malt liquor. Can you capture it?" Balthazar asked.

Christian concentrated on *feeling* the boyfriend's mind. It wasn't hard. It was like a red haze in the air. Red equaled violence and stupidity all at once. Christian reached for it mentally and *grasped* it. It was squishy and the boyfriend drew in a sharp breath before going almost limp.

"Don't squeeze," Balthazar warned. "You'll turn him into a vegetable. Just hold him as if you were gripping a thin piece of crystal stemware. He's hardly as expensive or as interesting, but he's *delicate*."

Christian frowned and lessened his mental grip. The boyfriend blinked and looked perplexed at Christian and Balthazar being in the apartment, but he wasn't violent. Just mildly annoyed. The girlfriend on the other hand was focusing on them with huge eyes. She was terrified. She opened her mouth to scream, but Balthazar put a finger to his lips and her mouth went lax. No scream issued.

"Now, he is truly yours to do whatever you want with, Christian. His mind is completely pliable. Whatever you want him to know or not know–"

"If we just drink from him–and *don't* kill him–will he hurt her again another day?" Christian asked.

Balthazar was silent for a moment. Christian didn't know if he was truly looking into the mind of the boyfriend or just relying upon his understanding of human nature. But finally, Balthazar said, "He will. He'll just kill her another day. Unless, of course, we alter their minds."

"Alter them in what way?"

"We give her the agency to leave him. We give him the belief that if he comes around her, something bad will happen to him." Balthazar shrugged.

Christian considered this. "I want to alter them. I mean I want *you* to alter their minds."

"Don't you want to try?"

"I don't think I want to scramble somebody's mind. Even this asshole's," Christian said.

"All right."

"Just all right?" Christian asked.

"I understand what you want. It is an easy fix." Balthazar shrugged again.

Christian felt an upwelling of outrage. But then he stopped himself as a revelation came to him. "You don't go after evil doers often, do you?"

Balthazar shook his head. "You come to find that there are endless amounts of them. The same dirty story played out again and again with victims needing the strength to leave and villains acting out of a rage they don't understand. Often it is because they were hurt when they were very young, other times they are just poison from the beginning."

"So you see it as *pointless?* To help one when there are so many others in the exact same spot?" Christian felt a wave of despair.

Were humans all so predictable and, worse, the *same?* Would he develop a laissez faire attitude towards them, too?

This time Balthazar cupped his cheek. "I will help them if you wish me to. Perhaps it will have a good effect. A ripple effect on others they will touch."

"I want you to help them," Christian said.

The two humans stood like empty dolls before them, unmoving, unseeing. Balthazar crossed to them. He went to the boyfriend first. He was none too gentle when he tipped the man's head to the side and bit into his flesh. The rich, coppery scent of blood flooded the room. Christian found himself leaning forward and his eyelids fluttering halfway shut as if he was a starving man that had smelled roasting meat. The boyfriend let out a sigh as Balthazar finished with him and let him sink to the ground.

Before Balthazar went to the girl, he leaned down and murmured something into the boyfriend's ear. The boyfriend's eyes widened, but then went dull again. He nodded. Christian knew he would not bother the girl again.

Christian barely registered when Balthazar went to the girl. He spoke to her first, much longer than to the boyfriend. Her gaze seemed empty for a long time, but then she gave one brief nod. Then he drank from her, too.

Balthazar then arranged the two of them. The girl he put in the bedroom and placed the thin coverlet over her. The boyfriend he put on the couch. The way he angled him, Christian was sure that it would be clear to him that he was to leave the girl without even speaking a word to her.

Christian's stomach felt like an empty sack, but he didn't want to feed in this desperate, terrible apartment that reeked of mold and bad memories. The Vampire Lord obviously felt the same way as he didn't try to embrace Christian to exchange blood. He and Balthazar stole out of the apartment the same way they had come. They slipped into the Mercedes convertible and raced out of town. Christian found he couldn't breathe until they were on the highway and far from that apartment.

The ride back to the manor took far less time–or so it seemed to Christian–and he was *so* glad. Tension bled from his shoulders the moment they pulled into the garage. The engine ticked once it was turned off. Balthazar–not speaking–took his hand and the two of them went into the garden. They sat down on a smooth wooden bench, which faced a wide swath of the sky. Though there was no sign of the sun, Christian knew it was coming. He turned towards Balthazar.

"Thank you," he whispered. "I know it's a drop in the bucket. I know it probably doesn't mean anything, but–"

"It means something to *you*. And that's all that matters." Balthazar stared at the sky, not looking at him.

Christian found himself leaning his head on Balthazar's shoulder. "We're each individuals. We each matter."

"Of course," Balthazar said, though Christian wasn't sure he truly agreed. The wind whistled through the trees and the scent of flowers flowed over them. "Are you hungry?"

"Starving," Christian admitted.

"All right. Let's feed you."

Balthazar began to fold back the sleeve of his shirt to offer him his wrist but Christian caught it and shook his head. He moved a hand to Balthazar's throat. He undid the buttons at Balthazar's chest until a large swath of the Vampire Lord's body was exposed. The scent of him was like the freshest snow and anise. Christian buried his nose against Balthazar's skin and just breathed in the Vampire Lord's scent. Balthazar shivered as if this was incredibly pleasurable.

Christian's fangs extended effortlessly and he slowly sank them into the tender flesh at the hollow of Balthazar's throat. Blood gushed into his mouth like hot, mulled wine. It poured down his throat as easily as water.

Balthazar cradled the back of his head as he fed. Christian swore he could feel the blood enter his every cell. They tingled. That tingling quickly swept between his legs and he was achingly hard, but though he was certain Balthazar was aware of it, the Vampire Lord did not take advantage. Balthazar's fingers just carded through his hair and his other hand stroked his back. He swore he heard Balthazar telling him all was well. All was safe.

He was loved.

Christian fell into a deep, dark sleep.

THE HEARER OF PRAYERS

*D*aemon slid out from underneath Julian. His fledgling made a sleepy objection that had the Vampire King petting the young man's hair and tucking him more fully underneath the soft down comforter. The coolness of the room, after the warmth of Julian and the luxurious mattress, had him shifting uncomfortably.

He longed to stay curled around his fledgling until Julian woke. He wanted to feel Julian nibbling on his throat. They would kiss languidly. A thin stream of blood would pass between them. Not enough to satisfy, but just to tease. This would lead to more rubbing together like the other night... or perhaps more. He longed to know Julian's body intimately in every way. But that led to those uncomfortable questions they had not settled.

Would they be lovers or just Master and fledgling?

Would they be monogamous?

Would they be *more*?

Perhaps then it was best that he needed to Commune with the Earth, with his skin touching soil and plants and grass. He needed to reconnect to this world after he'd been gone so long. It would remember him. Planets had memories that put Immortals' to shame.

This Communion would aid him in recovering his powers more

quickly. If Julian had been awake, Daemon suspected he would want to be utterly present with his fledgling and would neglect this necessary act. So it was definitely best that he let Julian sleep. Newly made fledglings needed far more sleep than older Vampires, let alone an Immortal such as himself. Even before the sun dipped below the horizon, he had been fully awake.

Despite his need to commune, he sat beside Julian though for a long while, one hand resting in the young man's soft hair. His mind was quiet. He was *content*. In this moment, finally having the one that was meant to be his all along, he knew a measure of peace he had never known before. He had no thoughts outside this moment. That would change, of course. He would want to know what happened to the other Immortals. He would want his full strength returned. He would be restive not having established himself among his people. But, for now, the ache that had plagued him for innumerable years was finally *satisfied*.

Julian. Julian. Julian. I hope you dream of good things. I hope you are at least half as content as I am.

He leaned down and kissed Julian's temple. Another sleepy sigh was his reward and he couldn't help the grin that crossed his lips. Julian was so very young and full of questions and excitement. He was impressed with how readily Julian had engaged in their blood-sharing the night before. He'd thought he would have to coax Julian to take even a sip. Even now there was a stain on his fledgling's skin around his mouth and down his chin to show how very *eagerly* he had drunk.

He recalled all too well Ashyr's first fledgling. She had refused to drink and nearly perished as the thought of consuming the life force of humans appalled her. She had felt it was cannibalism. No matter the pleasure it brought her, she had refused sustenance. She only succumbed when she reverted to a full predator and could not stop herself. She ravaged a whole village. It was a lesson about the Thirst. One must always listen to it or fall into madness. Julian, clearly, thought of feeding as something to be enjoyed, if not reveled in. While Daemon would have to warn him of it, he doubted that Julian would ever experience it.

This was good. Julian needed to be strong. He already wanted to be independent. Daemon would give him some room to move, but he was the Master and the king. He would protect and guide the young one on his proper course. Another lingering kiss on Julian's temple, leaving an imprint of the young man's skin on his mouth, and Daemon rose up from the bed. It was time he Communed.

He did not dress as his bare flesh needed to be in contact with the earth for the powering up process to work. Besides, his clothing had not yet been cleaned. He would have to see about getting more to wear from Balthazar. He was curious about these modern clothes. Not that they ever could compare to his own in Nightvallen. But still, with a fledgling of this time, he would need to learn its ways as well. Yet he had no sense of shame or conspicuousness about his body. So, without hesitation, he padded out of their suite and into the hallway of the coach house completely nude.

He was striding down the stairs when he met Arcius coming upstairs. Arcius jerked to a halt in mid-step. His gaze was riveted upon Daemon's groin. His eyes swung down to Daemon's feet then quickly up to his head. Arcius immediately tried to bow, but being on the stairs made this impossible. Daemon waved him off. It was unnecessary for such formality.

"My king, I was just coming to see if you require anything," Arcius stammered out. His gaze now was very firmly upon the ground, which Daemon found strange. Did he think he must avert his eyes? Some of his subjects did that, but Arcius already felt much closer than them. A guide in this brave new world. Even if he had *touched* Julian without permission. "Perhaps–perhaps you were wondering about *clothing?* We have a tailor scheduled to come later this evening. Also, we are having some ready to wear items in various sizes and styles being delivered."

"Is my nudity distressing to you in some way?" Daemon asked. Speaking out loud was tiresome, but to connect minds was actually tiring and he needed to conserve his strength.

"I... *no*, of course not. You are perfectly formed," Arcius hastened to say.

"Yes," Daemon agreed.

Arcius let out a strangled laugh and ran a hand across his forehead. "You sound so like Balthazar when you say that."

Daemon snorted. "I am sure he pretends to think well of himself no matter what the truth of the matter is. I am merely stating a fact. This body is meant to be pleasing to your kind."

Arcius' head jerked up. His mouth opened, but no words came out at first even though it was clear that a million questions raced through his mind. Daemon was beginning to suspect that these Vampires had no understanding of the Immortals. He was just as clueless as to how matters stood.

"Walk with me. I must Commune in the garden. We may speak between here and there," Daemon suggested.

The Vampire King crossed his hands behind his back at the wrists and proceeded past the goggling Vampire. Arcius quickly hurried after him. Daemon had the distinct impression the man *still* wanted to cover him up, but was resisting mightily.

Arcius was wearing a floor length black robe with heavy gold jewelry. Yet despite the ornateness there was a sense of modesty about the garment. He wondered if Arcius would rip it off his own body and offer it to him if Daemon asked. Unlike the others–especially *Balthazar*–Arcius had accepted him as king already and would do almost anything he asked. Because of this he must be careful.

"You said that your body was *meant* to be pleasing to us. Does that mean you have a different ah... body *originally*? We know nothing of your kind really. Only that you came to Earth–and not even exactly when–and choose the strongest among the humans to–"

"What we were, we are no longer," Daemon answered swiftly. "We adapted. Our souls swam through the dark until we found new hosts when our old hosts were incapacitated beyond repair."

"Hosts? Traveling? I have so many questions!" Arcius cried, but then bit his lower lip. "But I can see that you are not inclined to answer them."

"Not all of them. And not *now*." Daemon gave him a small smile.

That seemed to placate the man. Arcius drew his hands down the front of his robe and then hid them in his sleeves. This stance seemed to calm him further.

"I am sure you are not surprised by my interest, but there is a greater need for correct information than simply to satisfy my own curiosity," Arcius explained. "You see I don't even know where to begin. We have many *myths* about you and the other progenitors of the Bloodlines. Damaging ones."

They had just reached the foyer of the coach house. Two Vampires were standing there. It was the little fighter from the night before, William, and the one who listed his powers off in an awe-filled voice, Isabel. They had been speaking quietly with her fussing over him.

William still looked pale and distraught, likely not having fed last night because of being too upset, but also because Daemon had required so much from their Acolytes. He frowned at this. He was not pleased that he had taken so much from this House that was obviously struggling on its own. But there had been no other choice. He would start hunting tonight. Julian would surely enjoy it.

When the two of them caught sight of him, their mouths dropped open. He was truly surprised that nudity had such an effect on these modern day Vampires. Or perhaps, it was just *his* nudity that was doing this. He was uncertain. He would have to figure this out as he adored letting the night air caress his skin. Isabel immediately dropped to her knees once she regained her composure. She tugged at William to kneel, too, but he resisted her.

"We're to treat him as a *guest*, not a *god*, Isabel!" William hissed in annoyance, though he did give Daemon a worried look.

"You have already gotten into enough trouble with Balthazar," she reminded him. "Kneel!"

William was about to, but Damon held up a hand, shaking his head.

"I do not require anyone to kneel to me, especially those who do not believe in me," he said quietly.

William's silver eyes darted up to his face in surprise. "It's not that I don't believe in you! I mean you're right *here*." He paused, then said,

"You have all the powers that the stories say you're supposed to as well. I just..."

"Say nothing more, William!" Isabel cried frantically.

"I wish to hear what he has to say. It will not offend me," Daemon assured her.

"Of course, my king." Isabel *still* looked miserable though.

"Be very careful with your words, William," Arcius urged the child Vampire. He wasn't sure this was any better of an idea than Isabel did.

William stood very tall, which still did not even have the top of his head reaching Daemon's shoulder and said, "The Immortals used us to fight their battles without regard to our welfare. After we overthrew them, some of the ones that had fought in those battles were so–so *damaged* that they continued the abuses with their own fledglings. My old Master Roan Tithe was like that."

Daemon felt a sickness well up in his stomach. Fledglings were a *treasure*. They were not soldiers. They were companions. He had heard a little of this Vampire Roan Tithe, but he sensed that there was so much more that would cause him to hate the man. If he was not already struck down by Balthazar then he would have done it himself.

William's arms crossed over his chest and he shuddered as he said, "He did unspeakable things to us and the only person who stopped him was Balthazar. The Order did nothing. The other powerful House leaders did nothing. The Council did nothing. Only Balthazar stopped the–the things..."

Daemon wanted to tell him that there was no need to speak of the atrocities that were committed against him and the others, but his mouth remained stuck shut. He did not wish to interrupt the flow of William's words. William might need to speak these things and he needed to hear. As king, he was to have protected them, but instead he had slept.

The Vampire child's voice steadied then and he continued, "After that night, I determined that I would only follow those that had earned my loyalty and respect. I may have failed in that at times." He swept one hand through the air. "But I keep my promise to myself."

Daemon respected that. He had respected that William was willing to fight for his friends and House members no matter how unworthy they might have been of such loyalty. William had clearly believed they were worthy so he had stood up to an impossible to defeat enemy.

William's eyes met Daemon's, unblinking, as he challenged in a voice soft and low, but full of conviction, "So you might be king, you may be the First Among Equals, but that does not mean I will follow you. You said that you would have killed Heath and Selene for *less* than coming into Nightvallen and attacking Julian and Christian, but I wonder how *much* less? Are you a tyrant, too? Will you seek to abuse your power? Do you want slaves? Followers? Worshippers? Or are you like the king they write of in the stories that Arcius tells us who would raise us all up?"

Arcius tells stories of me? What kind I wonder?

Arcius and Isabel held themselves *very* still. This was the moment of truth. Who was he really? The king, yes. But what kind? That latter question was the one that William was asking. In his youth, he might have struck down this boy for speaking to him in such a direct way. But time had shown him that wisdom curbed one's acting out on foolish pride. And besides, he admired William all the more for standing up and stating what many others would simply be too frightened to ask.

He kept his gaze on William, softening his tone perceptibly, "I am *not* the king because I say I am. I am only the king if you recognize me as such. That recognition can never be earned by compulsion or force or violence. Not true recognition that you feel in your heart."

William's pink lips parted in surprise. He felt a wave of relief mixed with happiness flow through the other two. They had already believed him good or hoped he was.

He reached out with one hand towards William's cherubic cheek in a silent request to touch him. William tipped his head so that only the tips of Daemon's fingertips were touching his smooth as silk skin. He guessed that this was a success to touch William at all.

"But those are just words, William. Watch what I do and make up your own mind," Daemon said and stroked that tender cheek once before drawing his hand away. William was wounded. He had been abused. Daemon would have to win him over slowly. It might not work at all. But he would not harm this being more.

William curled his arms around himself, looking thoughtful, but still very uncertain. Daemon made a motion to Isabel to rise and care for William. She got to her feet and placed an arm around William's slender shoulders.

Daemon bowed and told them, "Have a good rest of your evening."

He then proceeded out of the coach house and into the garden with Arcius walking slightly behind him. He smiled wryly as, once again, every Vampire who caught sight of him nude froze in place before pretending this wasn't unusual.

"Arcius, where is a place in the garden I might Commune where I will be... inconspicuous?" Daemon asked as yet another couple of Vampires stared at his groin.

"I take back what I said about you being like Balthazar. He would have been *strutting* with all this attention," Arcius murmured.

Daemon snorted. "Perhaps I should send you in for my coat though I must Commune nude."

"I will be happy to fetch it after you're settled," Arcius offered.

Arcius then led him to a side garden filled with a small bubbling fountain that was still running despite the chill air. The grass was neatly raked free of leaves. The grass was cold against his knees and calves as he knelt down.

"Would you permit me the honor of praying with you after I get your coat?" Arcius asked.

"Praying? I am not praying, dear Arcius. I am restoring my power through connection to the Earth," Daemon answered. He paused for a moment and asked, "Who do you pray to, Arcius?"

Arcius lowered his head. "Though exiled, I still consider myself a Confessor of the Order and that means I pray to... well, to *you*."

Daemon was the one to go very still this time. He realized then, more than ever before, that he needed to understand this world. Finally, he said, "Please feel free to join me after you retrieve my coat." Arcius bowed and went to leave, but Daemon called him back,

"And, Arcius, can you begin to bring me any books, scrolls or documents that explain what happened with the other Immortals and the Vampires up to the present?"

Arcius nodded, but then, with a slight hesitation said, "I will bring you a–a *device* that will allow you access to a vast library. It is similar to one of the Wells in Ever Dark."

Daemon's eyebrows rose. "Humanity has come so far? Or have Vampires?"

"Both. Well, I'll leave you and return shortly," Arcius said with another bow and this time he disappeared into the rest of the garden.

Daemon laid his hands on his knees, palms towards the heavens, and let his eyelids shut. He then reached for the power of the Earth.

* * *

"Though exiled, I still consider myself a Confessor of the Order and that means I pray to... well, to *you*." Arcius' voice drifted over to Fiona.

Her heart began to race the moment that she heard him. She swallowed and kept her face neutral in expression as Confessors Donato and Sloan were looking to her to know how to react. And she didn't kid herself that one or both of them wouldn't be eager to report to Caemorn any misstep she made. Being emotional about Arcius would easily be considered a punishable offense by the prickly and precise Preceptor.

"Who is Arcius talking to? I don't recognize him as a member of House Ravenscroft," Donato asked from beside her.

They were on the roof of the nearest house to the Ravenscroft mansion. It was half a mile away, but she didn't dare go any closer, though the listening equipment and their own enhanced senses weren't giving them very clear feedback. Yet even here, she felt exposed though they had amulets that came from the Helm Bloodline so they should be invisible unless they moved.

Yet merely being invisible didn't mean they didn't give off scents that the House Ravenscroft Vampires could pick up on a stray gust of wind. But they needed to know what was going on in there. Yet she had been so overcome with just hearing Arcius again that she hadn't actually been listening–let alone analyzing–what he'd said or who he'd been speaking to. Fiona internally cursed herself.

Sloan added, "He said he prayed *to* this Vampire. And is the guy *naked?*"

Fiona repositioned her high powered binoculars to catch sight of this allegedly *naked* Vampire that Arcius was speaking to. Arcius had lovers of both sexes. So it was conceivable what they had arrived upon was a loving session. Why else would this other Vampire be naked?

Maybe just an exhibitionist? But she immediately discounted this. *An exhibitionist that Arcius prays to? He only prays to... to...*

Her binoculars focused on a single male, naked figure who was kneeling, perfectly still, on a rectangular section of grass near a fountain. Even from this distance, she could see the perfection of his form. He was big–as Arcius liked his men–but also lean of line. He had thick, black hair with natural waves. His features reminded her of Greek statues of the gods. His head was bowed and his eyes were closed. She suddenly wished very much that he would open those eyes. Arcius was nowhere in sight. He must have left. Another reason to curse herself for losing track of things.

"What the Hell?" Sloan hissed and there was a slight scraping sound as she moved on the roof.

Fiona grimaced and was about to caution her to be *silent* when she realized what had caused the woman to react in that way. Tendrils– red and glowing–were erupting from the earth all around this figure. They wound around the naked Vampire's body in a lover's caress. Their ends sank into his flesh and they began to pulse.

"What is *that?*" Donato gasped.

"It is like the Earth itself is giving him its life blood," Fiona whispered out loud.

And, at that moment, as if he had heard her, the Vampire's eyes opened. They were as red and glowing as the tendrils that surrounded him. He looked *right* at her.

Fiona grabbed the two Confessors by the napes of their necks and yanked them off the roof. They let out startled gasps as she launched them into the air. They fell the two stories to the ground, but each of them landed on their feet.

"Run," she told them, her heart in her throat. "Run as fast as you can."

The three of them rabbited into the darkness. She wasn't certain when it would be safe to stop running. She wasn't sure it *ever* would be.

Arcius would only pray to King Daemon. King... Daemon... That was him. Oh, by the Immortals, that was him!

FINE

Julian awoke feeling luxuriously lazy. His naked limbs were lax beneath the soft-as-a-cloud comforter. The mattress beneath him cradled his body. He stretched his arms over his head and pointed his toes. There were no aches or pains, just comfort. He drew an arm down the bed beside him, looking for something or really looking for *someone*. The mattress was cool. No one had lain there for some time.

Daemon was not there. Julian felt a subtle flutter of panic, but nothing major. Because he felt the Immortal in his head at that moment. Daemon was nearby. He was meditating. Communing was the word that was sent through their bond. Julian didn't bother him further. He could sense that Daemon was busy with this very important task. Everything was *fine*.

The flutter went away as if it had never been, but Julian wondered at it a little. He had never been afraid to be alone. Though he and Christian were inseparable, they didn't crowd one another. When they were researching, for example, they could be in different parts of Wingate, his parent's home, and not see one another for hours. He was never panicky about it. But Daemon not being there was unnerving.

Julian opened his eyelids and looked around him. The room should have been perfectly dark. There were no windows or lights on, but he could still see. It wasn't seeing in the usual sense. It reminded him more of when they used their night vision cameras and there was a slight greenish tinge to everything. That's what he saw now, but quite a bit clearer. He sat up. The comforter tumbled down into his lap and lay there like a fallen cloud. He rubbed his face with one hand and it came back gritty. There was something on his chin and lips. He should clean himself up and go find Christian.

With that in mind, Julian slid out of the bed. He pulled on a pair of silk pants he found on the bench at the end of the bed that must have been left by one of the Acolytes and padded towards where he remembered the bathroom being. He could actually smell the bath products–citrus and amber and rosemary–wafting out of the open doorway. He didn't turn on any lights until he stepped onto the cool tiled floor of the bathroom. He then looked at himself in the mirror.

Blood.

He stumbled back, not stopping until he hit the far bathroom wall and cold marble sucked all the warmth from his skin. His face, chin, throat and chest were smeared with dried blood. His lips and teeth were stained with it. Julian began to hyperventilate.

He slowly reached one hand up to lightly touch his chin, but his fingers sprang away as if they had minds of their own. He knew that this was simply the blood from last night's feeding frenzy. At the time, it had been amazing. He'd felt almost high from it. Not just almost, but definitely high, trippy, drugged out. But even before the blood exchange had gone on, before he'd lost himself in the ecstasy of the feeding, he'd known that he was going to drink blood. But somehow seeing the evidence of it all over his face and neck and chest was *different.*

I'm a Vampire, he thought. *I'm really a Vampire. I must drink human blood to survive.*

He both wanted and didn't want Daemon there at that moment. He kept his emotions and thoughts tightly inside his own mind. He wasn't sure how the Immortal would react to him freaking out about blood drinking. After all, that's what Vampires did. That's how they lived. That's how they survived. And it was pleasurable. More than pleasurable.

But it's reminding me now of what I thought about Vampires before... that they're monsters... that I'm a monster...

He closed his eyes for long moments. Daemon had fed from multiple people the night before. Even through the haze, he remembered those people being *fine* afterward. They had enjoyed being drunk from. The pleasure on their faces had surprised and pleased him. After the feeding, they had been carried out still alive and utterly well. Daemon had not killed them. Julian had not been a part of murder or death.

But it was still this knowledge that he was doing something that he would have considered disgusting just a few days ago that was rather shattering. He had gone with the flow, not really thinking too deeply about what he was doing. Maybe that was best. To just drift on the currents. Because, otherwise, he would have to admit that he had become the very thing that had killed his parents.

His eyelids flew open. Who had killed his parents? Balthazar? Someone in his House? Or maybe another Vampire he'd yet to even hear of? Was he just going to let their deaths go because he was now the same as the creature that had taken their lives?

He studied his red lips and pale skin beside it. He had never been very cognizant of his looks. He knew some people found him attractive. But when he looked into the mirror now he was more than that. His skin had this luminosity that it hadn't before. He stifled the urge to issue a snort of laughter. He did sort of *sparkle*. But the blood that covered the lower half of his face did not look romantic or sexy. He looked *inhuman*.

He heard a knock on the door and Arcius' voice calling out, "Julian?"

Julian opened his mouth to answer, but he couldn't. The words seemed frozen in his throat. Then the horror at the thought that Arcius would *see* him like this: covered in blood and... and... and...

He shut the bathroom door with Vampire quickness just as Arcius stuck his head into the main room. "Julian, are you all right?"

"I… I'm…" Julian shuddered. A full body shudder. He rested his forearms on the door's surface. How could the man appear now? Just when he was having a breakdown? It was like Arcius knew!

"Julian?" Concern tinted Arcius' voice.

He was much closer now. Just outside the bathroom door. Julian could picture him: big bearded face a few inches from the door, a concerned frown on his lips, and a creased forehead. He had to say something to get the man to go away.

"It's okay, Arcius. I'm just…" Julian went over to the sink and frantically turned on the faucet and tried to scrub the blood away. But there was so much of it. It didn't seem like he was making a dent. "Just washing up."

"Julian, it's all right," Arcius' voice was so gentle as if he knew what was happening. He clearly wasn't listening to what Julian was saying, but maybe how he was saying it. Who knew what harmonics a Vampire like Arcius could hear in his voice. "Please let me come in. I can help you."

Julian stared into his *purple*–sparkling purple with silver highlights–eyes and hardly recognized himself. He didn't look human. With the pale skin, violet eyes and blood stained mouth he looked like what he was: *Vampire*.

I'm going to have to get some contacts. No one is going to believe these are real.

He muffled a hysterical laugh with one hand. It ended up sounding a bit like a sob.

"Julian, I'm coming in now," Arcius said firmly. He'd clearly heard the sob.

Julian hadn't locked the door, but, even if he had, that wouldn't have kept a Vampire out, let alone one as powerful as Arcius, so he knew that the man was coming in. He stood, frozen, at the sink as Arcius stepped inside. Arcius' gaze met Julian's in the mirror. Julian's eyes were wide. Water dripped off of his chin. Red tinted water pooled in the sink's bowl. Arcius picked up a towel, wet it under the tap and started to tenderly clean Julian's face.

"I'm sorry," Julian breathed. "I don't know what's wrong with me."

Arcius looked into his eyes. "Don't you?"

Julian reached up to his face again, but dropped his hand once more. "The blood. I'm just... I'm a mess. I should shower."

He wanted to get under scalding hot water and *scrub*.

"And you will. After we talk a little bit," Arcius told him. He'd swabbed off Julian's face and his neck was next.

"There's nothing to talk about. I'm *fine*," Julian said, but his voice shook a little. He swallowed and firmed his lips.

Arcius gave him a quirky smile. "Why am I certain that you say this often? I bet that you have had to be *fine* for a lot of your life, haven't you?"

Julian turned his head, suddenly unable to meet Arcius' gaze any longer. His eyes burned with ridiculous tears and he blinked them away. "Normally, I am fine. And I *will* be fine. Just there's been a lot of changes over the last couple days. I just saw the blood and it all came... came flooding in. I don't know. Last night was *amazing*. I wanted what happened to happen. I don't know why I'm-"

"Freaking out?" Another smile. Tender and understanding. "Because nothing that has happened to you since this all began is normal."

"Even for a Vampire?" Julian gave him a jagged grin.

"*Especially* not for a Vampire." Arcius looked quite grave as he explained, "We prepare people for their Second Life with a great deal of care. They're tutored in Vampire society, laws and customs. They undergo psychological testing and counseling-"

Julian caught Arcius' wrist lightly, but much too fast for him to actually see. "Wait a minute! There are Vampire psychiatrists?"

"Of course," Arcius said so matter of factly that Julian was shocked into silence. But then he thought of Dr. Stone. The Vampires probably chose people for their skills and aptitudes. It made sense to him. "These potential fledglings are welcomed into the night after they have come to see the act of feeding as solely beautiful."

"It was beautiful," Julian murmured, remembering how his and Daemon's bodies had just melded together as they'd exchanged blood.

It felt like exchanging pieces of their *souls*. Other than with Christian, he'd never felt so close to anyone. He wondered what it would be like to exchange blood with his best friend. His chest clenched at the thought and he wasn't sure if it was in desire or disgust or a mixture of both. He rubbed his eyes. "If Christian saw me like this he totally wouldn't be surprised."

"How so?" Arcius asked as he continued to clean him as if it were totally normal for two adult men to bathe one another and have it be nothing sexual. But the truth was that Julian just felt very *safe* with the Vampire Confessor. He sensed–no, he *knew*–that he was not in danger from this big bear of a man.

"I'm always gung ho about things. Ready to try anything once. And, for the most part, I don't regret it." Julian gave him a wry smile. "But there are other times when I do something that's just a little bit more of a stretch for me and when I come down from the experience... It's not exactly a regret. It's just that I don't feel like myself."

He caught sight of his face in the mirror again. No longer was he covered in flaking dried crimson, but instead was clean and looked somehow *pure*, especially with his strange eyes. Arcius touched the skin beneath one of his eyes.

"Beautiful," Arcius murmured.

"But they set me apart even among Vampires," Julian guessed.

The Confessor nodded. "But I do not imagine that you ever cared to fit in."

"No, I never have. But I have a feeling that this may make things more difficult for House Ravenscroft."

Arcius nodded again. "But it is something we must do. It is not something we can shirk from. And, I think, in the end, it will lead to good." The bear-like Vampire shook himself. "We have gone a little off topic. We must talk about *you* and all of this."

"I'm good now." Julian held a hand out to show that he was steady as a rock. He only felt a little fragile, but he could hide that.

Evidently, he was losing his touch at lying or Arcius was just a really good observer as the Confessor gave him a disbelieving look of furrowed brows and compressed lips.

"You went from not even knowing we existed–or worse, believing we did, but *hating* us–to suddenly being one of us. More than one of us. The fledgling of the First Among Equals," Arcius pointed out. "And that's just the start of what's happened to you, isn't it? You were attacked. You thought your best friend was going to die. You then experienced your first feeding last night–one of the most unusual ones that I have ever experienced–and you claim to be *fine*. Is that about right?"

"I think that just about sums it up." Julian nodded and let out an inappropriate laugh.

Arcius' expression grew troubled. "And then you woke up alone–"

"This isn't Daemon's fault!" Julian found himself defending the Immortal.

"Fault? No. Not understanding what a fledgling needs? What a former *human* needs?" Arcius didn't answer these questions out loud, but Julian could see the answers in his eyes.

"He's communing... or something. It's important!"

"And that is why I am not bringing him in here at this instant," Arcius answered.

"You would drag him in here by his ear?" Julian gave a disbelieving smile. "I thought you worshiped him or something."

"He is our progenitor," Arcius intoned as if this were a school room. "He holds answers to questions we haven't even thought to ask about ourselves. He has lived countless ages. He has much wisdom to impart. And, from all I have seen of him, he is worthy of respect... and worship. But that does not mean he is infallible."

"He's not. I mean he's great, but he's not perfect." Julian looked down at his bare feet. His toes gripped the cool tile. "But I know that he wouldn't do anything to hurt me. We're figuring this fledgling thing out together. And I'm cool with–with what he's doing."

Julian felt like he was protesting too much on Daemon's behalf. He remembered that faint panic. He firmed his shoulders. He wasn't a child any longer. Daemon was not his parent. He could stand on his own two feet. He had gone to countless countries around the world, entered night shrouded tombs, run from men with guns, climbed snow-chilled mountains, spelunked in forgotten caves, scuba dived over one hundred feet down, and so much more. He *wasn't* a wilting flower. How could he be so much stronger as a Vampire, but feel weaker in this one thing, at least, than he had as a human?

"And I am guessing you are hiding from him these turbulent feelings you are experiencing?" Arcius looked rather stern.

"I'm fine… now."

Arcius gave out a long suffering sigh. Somehow that made Julian feel warm inside. He imagined that Arcius made this sound often with those he cared for.

"You are Daemon's *first* fledgling. Though he witnessed the other Immortals create their own, he would not know exactly what to do," Arcius explained. "He is still new at this. He needs guidance."

"And you're going to give it to him?"

This had another, genuine smile dawning on Julian's lips. He could well imagine the bear-like Vampire, hands on hips, telling Daemon to go cuddle with his fledgling or else! It was a ridiculous image, one that would never happen, but it cheered him nonetheless.

"I will give him my advice. I just took him to the garden and came back here to get him his coat. I think you should accompany me to see him," Arcius told him as he finished off drying Julian's chest with another towel.

Julian frowned even as his heart rate sped up a little at seeing Daemon. "He loves that coat though, really, he needs some modern styled clothes. At least the fur is warm."

"Yes, he is quite fond of it." Arcius' tone was dry as he reminded Julian, "Vampires don't feel the cold as humans do. And I think that Daemon may feel it even less. He's out there right now… *naked.*"

It took Julian a few beats to understand what Arcius. His eyebrows crawled up into his hairline. "*Naked?* Outside in the garden?"

"Yes."

"He just walked on out there with you to the garden totally *naked?*" Julian really had to understand things.

"Yes."

"Okay."

"Indeed."

"Vampires are probably beyond modesty and all that. I mean... right?" Julian asked.

Yet at the same time, Julian had the ridiculous urge to stomp out into the garden with a very large blanket and wrap Daemon in it. He also had an equal urge to start laughing uproariously as Arcius, on the one hand, didn't seem phased, but, on the other, seemed scandalized at the same time.

"We are. Though some are more modest than others." Arcius paused, then added, "I think it is simply surprising, because seeing Daemon, unclothed, is, well, *worshipful.*"

That had Julian's eyebrows rising again. Then he admitted, "He's really hot. I mean *really.*"

"He is perfection and he is our progenitor and the First Among Equals and–"

"It's like royalty walking around nude in front of the subjects, right? Something like that?" Julian clarified.

"In fact, royals *did* many things nude in front of their servants–"

Julian held up a hand. "I don't want to know. Let's see what we do about our particular royal and this nude thing."

"Why do you not brush your teeth and finish freshening up while I get his robe?" Arcius suggested.

"Sounds good," he answered.

Julian thought of the scalding shower he had wanted to take. But he didn't feel the need for it right at that moment. Maybe he'd take a shower with Daemon later. He was really *fine* now or well on his way to it.

Arcius had turned and was heading out the door when Julian called out to him, "Arcius?"

The Confessor turned with a raised eyebrow. "What?"

"T-thank you." Julian grimaced and rubbed a hand through his hair. "Thank you for checking on me and cleaning me up and talking and... all of it."

"There is no need for thanks. In a House, we support one another," Arcius said with another kind smile.

"Yeah, but Daemon and I aren't House Ravenscroft," Julian hated saying that, but it was true.

Arcius spoke carefully, "In a way, you are of *every* House and Bloodline, Julian. Being Daemon's fledgling you are connected to us all and should be welcomed by us all."

"Thanks." He looked down at his scrunched toes again. He wondered if anyone other than Arcius felt this. But, at least, the Confessor did. Being close to Christian's House was utterly important to him. They were now in this literally *forever*. "That means a lot."

Arcius nodded and went out. Julian headed back to the vanity. There was a wrapped toothbrush and fresh toothpaste. His mouth was the last place where he could still see the pinkish stains. He opened his lips and looked inside. His fangs came out after a moment. It was so odd to see them elongate. They slid out of his gums easily before retracting again.

Okay, that's going to take a little getting used to. But I can do it.

He brushed his teeth and washed his face again. He leaned on the vanity for another moment before leaving the bathroom. He had to appear like he was totally on top of his game. He didn't want to freak out anyone else, especially not Daemon or Christian.

He didn't want his best friend trying to take care of him when Christian was, undoubtedly, going through similar experiences or perhaps even worse. Christian didn't really like change at all. He didn't like things out of his control. Everything that had happened to them recently was a whole lot of change and little in their control. He simply didn't want to burden Christian.

He pushed off the vanity and went into the living room where Arcius was waiting for him. Slung over one arm was Daemon's luxurious fur coat with the high collar. In his other hand he had a pair of slip-on shoes and a shirt for Julian. Julian took them from him and put them on swiftly. If they were going to chastise Daemon for walking around in the buff they had to be covered up.

After he stuffed his feet into the shoes, the two of them swiftly left the coach house. He felt other Vampires in the area, but they seemed to stay away from him. Maybe they thought that Daemon's fledgling would also walk around nude and worried the Vampire King might take exception to them seeing him naked. Julian's mouth quirked into a half-hidden grin.

When Arcius opened the door and the cool fall air wrapped around him, Julian realized that he really wasn't bothered by the cold. When he'd been in the derelict parking garage, he hadn't felt it either, but he was so out of sorts then that he hadn't been sure if this would last. Now he knew.

Arcius took him to a small, isolated garden where he'd left Daemon. Julian's steps went faster as they got nearer the Vampire King. He could feel with every step that his master was near. He swallowed and stepped past some bushes only to come to a screeching halt. Arcius walked straight into him.

"Julian, what–oh my!" Arcius' voice dropped to an awe-filled whisper.

It was Daemon. Or rather the cage of glowing crimson vines that encircled his naked form. He was sitting cross-legged, hands on knees, palms facing to the heavens and these vines wrapped around every limb, every finger even. The tips of them were inserted into Daemon's flesh. There was a *wave* of light that started from the roots where the vines came out of the ground that moved into Daemon's body. Julian could have sworn he saw that light wave move through Daemon's body. It was so *alien* a sight, but it was also beautiful. Julian wasn't sure how long he and Arcius watched this before speaking.

"So this is Communing," Julian breathed.

"I thought–thought he was simply going to pray or meditate. I did not know... I did not know it would be *this*," Arcius admitted and the Confessor seemed stunned–and awed–down to his bones.

At that moment, Julian felt Daemon's mind reach for him. It was as if Julian, too, was enmeshed in those vines of light. His eyelids fluttered shut as this sense of well being flowed through him. The tension he hadn't known he carried washed away.

My fledgling, you were frightened and thought yourself alone, Daemon's voice rolled through his mind, filled with regret and tenderness. *Forgive me. I did not think you would wake before I came to get you.*

It's okay. I'm... fine, Julian sent.

Oh, you are such a strong warrior, but I can see your heart. There is no shame in this. I missed you, too. And in this strange, new place, I will need your company, Daemon assured him.

And there was an accompanying mental caress. Julian let out a shivery sigh. The pleasure of being embraced and caressed like this could not fully be put into words. It made him feel stronger and weaker than ever before, because it showed him... *himself.*

You have it. I just don't want to burden you or Christian or anyone, Julian admitted.

You are not a burden. You are a joy, Daemon said and Julian swallowed hard. *But, before we Commune together, you must tell Arcius some news.*

What is it? Julian was curious.

We are being watched.

Daemon told him about the three Vampires he had seen. He especially described a beautiful black woman who had appeared to be in charge. Julian opened his eyes only to find Arcius glancing between himself and Daemon.

"You were speaking to him?" Arcius asked.

Julian nodded. He felt a little *distanced* from his body and the rest of the world. He was still enmeshed in the Vampire King's mental embrace, but he had to tell Arcius this news. So he did. With every word, Arcius' awe was replaced by alarm. Finally, at the description of the beautiful black woman, his expression grew grim.

"You know her?" Julian asked.

Arcius nodded. "Stay with Daemon. I must go speak with Balthazar. The woman you saw is a powerful, influential Confessor. If she knows about Daemon then Preceptor Caemorn Losus knows as well."

"And that's not a good thing?" Julian guessed.

Arcius looked grimmer still. "No, not at all."

EYROS

Balthazar was smiling. It was a *huge* smile that actually had his face aching a little bit. But he couldn't help it. The night before Christian had fed from his throat willingly! And this night, Christian had seemed pleased to see him when he'd checked in on his fledgling in Christian's bedroom.

When he'd knocked on Christian's bedroom door that evening, Christian had called for him to come in. He'd found his beautiful, particular fledgling about to get in the shower. Not undressed alas, but in a pair of sleep pants and a t-shirt. Balthazar had not ogled. It was tough, but he'd managed to keep his gaze on Christian's *face*. Not that this was necessarily difficult, mind you, as he adored that face, with the blond curls flowing over the noble brow and glittering silver eyes. But still…

Yet he was rewarded for his innocent behavior by Christian promising to join him later. He'd promised with a *smile*. Balthazar manfully further resisted the urge to ask if he could join Christian in the shower. He was quite proud of himself that his face had remained a placid mask. Yet Christian had given him a slight narrow-eyed glance at one point as if he guessed what was on the Vampire Lord's mind. But Christian's mood had not soured towards him so that was all right then.

There would definitely be more feeding tonight as Christian needed to be fed every cycle. Maybe another sip from his throat. Maybe another *kiss*... Now, he only had to figure out if they had to hunt again or if Daemon had left any of the Acolytes in any state to be fed from by others. He actually was hoping that they had to go on a hunting trip again. That had seemed to make them closer. Christian loved to learn and teaching him was a pleasure.

Maybe he should take Christian to the Mirryr Blood Den that night. House Margolies of the Mirryr Bloodline wanted him to look into the minds of some humans they were thinking of taking on as Acolytes. He often did this in order to get favors from the other Houses. Being exiled from the Ever Dark meant that they didn't get their share of the technological or magical goodies any longer. At least not directly. But since Balthazar had the best success in choosing Acolytes that could be trusted and later turned, the other Houses would pass some along.

His success came, in part, from the fact that he could simply compel the humans to be trustworthy on a deep, subconscious level. Though there were always somewhere that compulsion wouldn't be as successful that meant they were intent on causing trouble and should be weeded anyway.

This service had paid off in spades. Though with Daemon now a guest in his House, and Nightvallen potentially open to them, he wondered how much they would need these other Houses any longer. But, then again, Daemon had quite the appetite and potential needs so he would keep all lines of communication open.

Yet thinking of Daemon and Acolytes made him think of Rey. His mouth flattened again. They would have to replace Rey. Maybe tonight, he could also start to look for prospective candidates. He wondered how Christian would take to that task. He thought that Christian might be a natural at reading people, but he knew that his fledgling still wasn't comfortable with the whole idea of Acolytes.

It was as he was making his way down the south hallway that he noticed members of his House clustered together, looking at their phones or tablets. They quickly lowered them as soon as they saw him and pretended to have not been looking at them at all. This suspicious activity had him frowning. He'd left his phone in his room, finding it best to spend as much time unplugged as he could.

He had discovered, much to his annoyance, that he could easily become addicted to sleek and shiny electronics so he chose not to have them on him at all times. But, clearly, something was fascinating to his people. He saw Riley up ahead. She had hardly left her mistress' side since she was struck down—yet another thing he had to do was visit Elena—and he noted that the teenage Vampire looked a little paler than she should. He would have to force her to eat.

But then he noticed that Riley, too, had quickly hid her phone. That meant one thing. They were using the app that Riley had designed and he had forbidden them to use. Well, he hadn't forbidden it exactly, but the deal was that no electronic device was to record anything about Vampire kind. The app that Riley had put together didn't record, but only live streamed to House Ravenscroft, but there were so many ways that could go really wrong.

Enough is enough, he thought.

"Show me what's so interesting to all of you." He extended his arm towards her and wiggled his fingers.

She made a faint grimace then she got out her phone and tapped on one of the icons before handing it to him. She quickly said, "It's not being recorded anywhere and it's only for the House. No one else can see. So it's perfectly secure. I know you don't like it, but–"

"Nothing is *perfectly* secure. You've told me that yourself." He took the phone from her, more alarmed now than simply interested.

What he saw on the screen made no sense to him at first. It was Daemon surrounded by *glowing tentacles*?! Was his guest being attacked? His head jerked up. "Where is this? How could you be watching this and not helping him?"

"He's in the garden! It's okay! He's just Communing is what Arcius told us. It's a natural thing. Crazy, right? I mean we're Vampires. Last thing I thought we had was a connection to the

Earth! Arcius didn't want Daemon to be crowded so Cicely is
streaming it."

"Tell her to stop! Right now! And no one is to send this out to
anyone!" he shouted.

"Okay, but I told you it can't be recorded–"

Balthazar was halfway down the hall as she called the last part
after him. "Riley! Just do it!"

Secrecy was key for the survival of his House not to mention
Daemon and Julian's safety! All it would take was for one of his
House in a religious fervor to take a screenshot or record Daemon
and send it out to other Vampires and all would be lost.

He broke into a run. He burst out the back doors into the garden
and headed to the small side garden where it had looked like Daemon
was Communing or being killed by tentacles or whatever. As to which
was correct, he estimated it was six of one, half a dozen of the other.

He found Arcius and Julian talking while Daemon was still on the
ground with the red glowing vines all around him. It was clear from
their behavior that Daemon was *fine* despite this bizarre and almost
beautiful display. Balthazar found that he had to tear his gaze away
from the softly pulsing vines. He was getting lost into an almost medi-
tative state from simply looking up on them.

Instead, he focused on the other Vampires in the garden. Cecily
was just pulling down her phone and stopping the livestream to the
House. Riley had done as he asked. Sophia Strange was also there, her
hands linked together behind her lower back, dressed in one of her
adorable anime girl outfits of pink polka dotted dress, cute boots and
perfect hair. She was rocking from side to side as she watched
Daemon with a small smile on her lips.

Cecily–her platinum blonde hair in pigtails–with big silver eyes
rather like a china doll's guiltily looked over at him. "I'm sorry, Balthazar!" Her whispery voice rose as loud as it normally ever got.
"Daemon said it was okay to watch and–"

Balthazar put up a hand to silence her. Daemon had no idea what
streaming or social media or anything like that was. He also seemed
to have no clue that he needed to be on the down low. He seemed

ready to announce to the whole goddamned world–Vampire *and* human–that he was back to rule them all. Even though Vampires didn't get headaches, Balthazar swore he felt one coming on.

At that moment, Arcius came over to him, leaving Julian crouched at Daemon's side. He watched as the young man brushed his fingers over one of the glowing tentacles that reached up through the earth. It actually unfurled from where it was around Daemon's body and curled around Julian's fingers. Julian's face lit up with amazement. Cecily covered her mouth with one hand, going back to watching with rapt attention, her phone forgotten at her side. Balthazar could already feel the rest of his House wanting to be in her position and watch, too.

"Balthazar, thank goodness you're up," Arcius said, which had Balthazar's head snapping towards him.

"I see I was missing a show," Balthazar responded rather tartly.

The truth was that what he was seeing was amazing to him, too. And it just proved how different Daemon was from the rest of them. He wasn't just some really old Vampire, he was an Immortal. He was likely *the* Immortal.

Arcius looked over at Daemon and this ridiculously happy expression, almost beatific, spread across his bearded features. "Yes, this is most certainly something not to be missed."

"And that's why you gave permission to Cecily to use the *forbidden* app?" Balthazar raised one eyebrow. Normally, the eyebrow raise had people in his House cowering, but not Arcius.

Arcius didn't even notice, but said absently, "I thought it was an important enough occasion for a little loosening of the rules."

Balthazar fought the urge to grab the Confessor by the front of his priestly robes. "Arcius, this–this *display* is going to cause the more religiously minded of our group to–"

"To *believe*?" Arcius focused on him again.

"To *tell*. What they're seeing... What they *think* they are seeing is proof of all the Order has said about the Vampire King! They'll want to share the good news! The only way to keep these two safe is to keep them secret!" Balthazar hissed. Arcius' bearded face went very serious and he lowered his eyes from Balthazar, which had him wondering what *else* he had missed while mooning over Christian. "What? Just tell me and get it over with! I don't want the bad news coming in dribs and drabs!"

"The Order already knows they are here," Arcius mumbled.

"*What*?!" Balthazar's voice was a bare whisper.

"Fiona and the two Confessors who attacked Julian in the Siryn Blood Den were watching us from the Gioges house." Arcius jerked his head towards the home just a mile and a half away.

Balthazar let out a string of curse words. "I *knew* I should have bought that place, but we didn't have the money to expand and there was no reason to believe–"

"This is not your fault. There was no way of knowing any of this would have happened. And besides, Fiona would have found a way to spy upon us," Arcius interrupted him gravely. "I trained her myself. She was a prodigy. Like you." There was a faint smile aimed at him under that beard.

"But I won you in the end and she's never forgiven me for that," Balthazar found himself saying.

"You did not win me. I went with you because this was where I was most needed," Arcius reminded him.

"I won you in *her* mind, Arcius. Whatever benign cast you wish to place this in, it does not matter. What she thinks does," Balthazar pointed out and scrubbed his face with both hands.

This was bad. Impossibly bad. If he was to have an arch enemy it would be Fiona Darksilver and what an arch enemy she was! Intensely intelligent, driven and zealous in her beliefs, she would never give up on a task, especially not one given to her by the Order. By Caemorn Losus.

"Was she just watching you for fun or do you think that Caemorn was behind this?" He asked this, but he already knew the answer.

If this had been some kind of lovesick viewing of her former mentor, she would have done it alone. She wouldn't have brought two other Confessors with her, especially not the same ones that had attacked Julian. All of this, from the deaths of Heath and Serena to the disappearance of Timothy made him realize that the Order had continued to watch him despite the exile. That sense of being in a fishbowl angered him.

When Arcius opened his lips to speak, Balthazar waved him off. "Don't answer that. I know she was here for Caemorn. Where is she now? Can we intercept her?"

"There is no need for that," it was Sophia who spoke in that sweet, little girl voice of hers. She had walked up to them on silent feet and was standing there, still swaying with that peculiar smile on her lips. "You don't need to be afraid.

Balthazar's eyebrows crawled into his hairline. *"Really?* And why is that?"

"Because this is how it is supposed to go." She beamed, her eyes closing as she was smiling so hard. "This is the beginning of the end of the beginning."

"Okay." He turned back to Arcius, not trusting Sophia to make sense. He doubted that Seeyrs ever really did. Seeing the future was bound to drive a person mad. It had clearly sent Sophia around the bend long ago.

"I know you don't believe me," she said, still beaming. "But you will!"

Balthazar didn't answer this. Instead, he was raking his fingers through his hair as he thought of the compound being rushed by who knew how many Confessors. Despite them being priests, they were trained for combat. The Order saw itself as warriors first and foremost for the faith.

How ironic that they want to destroy the person that they worship. But a dead god is so much easier to control than a pesky live one who might not share their ideas about how things should be. And, god forbid, might want to run things himself. He glanced at Daemon and frowned. Whether he believed in Daemon or not, the Order clearly did.

"Arcius, we need to prepare for an attack. I don't know–"

"There is no need to fear a large-scale invasion," it was Daemon who spoke. His voice was so arresting despite Balthazar's best attempts not to admire it.

135

Both he and Arcius turned to look at the Vampire King. Daemon began to stand.

At that same moment, Christian came jogging up to him. "What's going on Balthazar? The House is all in an uproar. Nobody's gone after Daemon or Julian again, have they? Oh, my God!"

That was the moment that Christian caught sight of Daemon, rising up, naked but still covered in the crimson vines. They all watched as the vines broke apart into embers. The red embers drifted up into the night sky.

"Beautiful," Arcius murmured.

Balthazar had thought many things about being a Vampire, but while he had thought that Vampires could be beautiful, he didn't think of them as bringing many beautiful things into the world. They were creatures of death. But this... *this* proved him wrong. And he wasn't sad about being wrong at all. Christian laced their fingers together as he continued to stare at Daemon. Looking down into his fledgling's face, he could tell that Christian felt it was beautiful, too.

When the last of the vines had disappeared and the embers were too far away to see any longer, Julian slid that ridiculous fur coat onto Daemon's naked form. The man was built, he'd give him that. He also had to reluctantly admit that Daemon somehow appeared *kingly* even when he was naked with a fur coat on. Daemon brushed his knuckles over Julian's cheek before giving him a sweet kiss. Julian looked a little dazed after the kiss, but Balthazar admired the fact the young man got his composure back right away. Julian knew that important things were happening and he had to be clear.

Of course, he would be like this. Christian is his best friend after all.

"Why do you say that there will be no invasion?" Balthazar got out, his voice only catching slightly.

"Because, if they intended to storm this location they would have come directly to the front gate to speak with you. But they choose secrecy," Daemon said then continued, "And from what Arcius tells me, the Order has made me into a hero to Vampires. Worshiping me is where they gain their power over the others, do they not?"

Balthazar glanced up at Arcius who was still staring at Daemon as if he couldn't quite believe all of this was real. As if a dream had come true. Balthazar sighed and squeezed the top of his nose.

"Yeah, that would be the short of it," he agreed.

"So they will not want many to know I am actually here, let alone that they wish to attack me in order to keep their own power base," Daemon said logically.

"No, I suppose they wouldn't."

"They will want to keep this as secret as possible. They will send people, their best people, but it will not be a strike force of any proportions," Daemon went on.

"They won't," it was Sophia who spoke in her clean, high voice. "The real battle will be in Solace. You will take the war to Caemorn. I believe that may be where my mistress is."

"You think Seeyr is in Solace?" Daemon asked her, one eyebrow rising.

"It is the only place I have not been able to get into," she answered without prevarication.

"So *that's* why you go from House to House," Balthazar muttered.

"Yes, of course. I am not one for change. As I told you, I am very happy to have found my forever home with you." She took his and Christian's bound hands and squeezed them with her own.

His fledgling was looking at her with a half-fond, half-confused expression that Balthazar was sure was on his own face. She was like a pet who had finally been chosen.

"Well… you know we are honored to have you," Balthazar told her.

"Aw! You're so sweet!" She gave him one of those eye-closing, beaming smiles again.

Balthazar turned back to Daemon. "You're likely right that they won't come en masse, but they will come. I need to bulk up our defenses. You're not at full power, I take it?"

"No, though I am much better than I was," Daemon answered.

Daemon had slid an arm around Julian's shoulders. Balthazar noted that Julian and Christian were looking at one another, and some silent, best friends' connection was going on there. He was sure they'd be talking between themselves, heads together, soon enough.

"I am actually strong enough to give you a *gift*. Your whole House a gift," Daemon said.

Balthazar frowned even as something inside him tingled. Could it be some technology or magic from Ever Dark? Could it be access to Nightvallen right this moment?

Balthazar found himself asking about the latter, "Would it not be safer for us to go to Nightvallen while you recover your full strength? Then when you're ready we can sally forth against all enemies."

He said "us" and not just Daemon and Julian. He would not have himself or his people left as sitting ducks for Confessors to come pick off. Daemon shook his head.

"I cannot return to Nightvallen at this time. My strength must be established here," he said simply. "The gift I will give you is of *oneness*."

"*Oneness?*" Balthazar's eyebrows crawled into his hairline again. What the Hell was oneness? Was it bogus?

But Sophia did know what it was. She clapped her hands together and jumped up and down. "Really? You're going to do that? You think he's ready?"

Daemon smiled indulgently at her. "I think Balthazar is *worthy*, don't you?"

She nodded. "Yes, yes, I do!" She turned shining eyes upon Balthazar. "Oh, this is so amazing! You're so lucky and blessed for him to do this!"

Balthazar turned towards Arcius, his brow furrowed with even greater confusion. The Confessor looked confused, too, which made him feel a little better.

"What is oneness?" Julian asked Daemon.

"I will explain, but first, I must bring everyone here so that they can understand what I am about to do as well," Daemon answered him.

And then there was this *thrum* in the air. Balthazar almost wanted to run to Daemon's side at that point, but he was able to resist it as he was already only a few feet away. But the rest of the House came rushing to them. Soon, every bit of the garden was filled with the shining silver eyes of Vampires.

Daemon gestured for Balthazar to stand beside him. Balthazar tugged Christian with him. Whatever this gift was, he wanted Christian to partake in it, too. As a new fledgling, Christian was still very weak and needed all the power he could get.

When they reached Daemon's side, the Vampire King began to speak, "I wish you all to know how grateful I am for your welcome and your hospitality. I would never repay your kindness with danger of any sort. But there are those who do not wish for my return."

Balthazar saw nodding heads all around. He was a little leery of Daemon telling all his House about the danger, but really, it had to be done. He was going to have done so himself at the meeting he was to have after this.

"While I am not at full strength, I am a formidable opponent, especially against those who do not believe in me and underestimate what I can do," Daemon continued.

Considering that had *just* happened last night in their front room, Balthazar tended to agree.

"But I am not at each of your sides during every moment. You need to be strong against those who would attack you to get to me," Daemon said and there was a tenseness in the crowd "That is why I wish to offer you something that will aid you in fighting any enemy: the strength of each other."

It seemed to Balthazar that all the Vampires were holding their breaths.

"I know some of the abuses that Master Roan Tithe inflicted upon you. I know how brave and strong that Balthazar had to be to free you from the yoke of his oppression. And I know how loyal you are to Balthazar for this great act," Daemon intoned.

Balthazar shifted uncomfortably. He never liked to think of Roan and he tended to like even less thinking of what he'd had to do. It didn't seem brave to him. Just necessary. He was fighting for his own life.

"This House exists because of that bravery, strength and loyalty. I think you should have an additional *reward*."

Daemon made a gesture with his right hand and abruptly those same glowing vines that had encased him erupted from the earth in front of each of them, including Balthazar, Christian, Arcius and Sophia, but excluding Daemon and Julian. The vines remained quiescent though Balthazar felt their readiness to do *something*.

"By allowing these vines to sink into your flesh, you will be sealing your House, not just with your loyalty, but with your blood. Each of you will have the strength of each other in battle. No longer will you be alone," Daemon explained. "I know how Vampires hoard their own power, and this will not take away from you, it will only add. It will make it so that House Ravenswood will have the strength of oneness like the great Houses in the past did."

Daemon seemed to meet every one of their gazes. Whatever he saw there, he approved of. Balthazar could feel his House's approval of this move. He, too, felt an eagerness for this. This oneness was something that he'd heard about in stories, and not under that name, but had thought was a myth. Evidently, it was not.

"All who wish to be a part of this need simply extend their hands. I will do the rest," Daemon informed them.

Balthazar was pleased to see that every member of his House extended their hand. He and Christian did the same, other hands still linked, at the same time. The vines immediately wrapped around each of their wrists. The sensation was strange. The vines were smooth and warm, almost rubbery in texture, but then their tips slid into his flesh and he gave a little gasp of pain. That was razor sharp.

But the pain was all but forgotten when he suddenly had the sense of every one of his House members. It was as if all their minds were pressed against him in warm mental embraces. He felt Arcius' bear-like strength, Sophia's amazing intellect, Riley's inquisitiveness and Christian's amazingly beautiful mind.

Power swelled up inside of him like a rising tide. It seemed to cover him, fill him, overtake him. All of his House was with him. He was with them. And he felt the blood—the Eyros blood—in their veins and he—he—

Daemon's hand was suddenly on his shoulder. His red-eyed gaze met Balthazar's. *Calm yourself. Calm. Do not reach for them yet. You are not ready, old friend. I will help you find your way.*

Balthazar blinked and he saw that the vines had done that breaking-apart-and-turning-into-embers thing again and were drifting away. All the Vampires in the garden were laughing and talking and crying and joyous and awed. They'd had this experience that had drawn them all together. He'd had it, too, but there had been something *more*. Something that Daemon had stopped him from reaching. Christian was looking at him concernedly. Balthazar gave Daemon a quizzical look.

"What did you mean by calling me an old friend?" Balthazar asked him.

Daemon did not speak out loud. He spoke into Balthazar's mind alone. *I should have recognized you. I am sorry I didn't. I blame the insanity of this awakening. I hope you will forgive me... Eyros.*

FROM BLUE TO RED

⤜

*C*aemorn grinned as he rode deeper into Solace's woods on his steed Neboa. Neboa was the color of mist and ran as fast as the rain storms that sometimes lashed the Order's city. The twin werewolf brothers, Tarn and Farun, whom he had sealed in their werewolf forms, flanked him. Their tongues lolled out to taste the air. They were on a *hunt*.

Caemorn adjusted his grip on the long spear known as Borage. The spear glowed with a soft blue-white light and that glow would increase the closer it was to the wielder's chosen prey. He'd found it in the armory in the Spire. There were many powerful, magical weapons there that Seeyr's people had, for some unknown reason, not used in their fight against the Order so long ago. The weapons were powerful, but also dangerous to the user. Many Vampires had died trying to wield them, but there were a few weapons like Borage that could be used without any fear. Yet he was certain that Seeyr and her people would have known the ways the others could have been used safely.

He saw Borage glowing hotter in his hand and knew that his prey was near. He had been tracking a creature known as a Night Hag for the past two hours. The creature looked like an elderly woman swathed in ancient tattered robes, but she could spring great distances and ran like the wind. Her fingertips were blackened, poisonous claws. The long, yellowed toenails on her feet could disembowel a man in three seconds flat.

The Hags favorite prey were the humans that were brought into Solace as the Order's food source. Young girls were a seeming delicacy for the dessicated creatures. Many loathed leaving the Ever Dark for Earth any longer–Caemorn was among those, preferring the peace and eternal darkness of Solace to the smelly, dirty, noisy world of the humans–so their food was brought to them.

Normally, the beings that lived in the Ever Dark stayed away from the city, but not the Hags. They were attracted to life. They drank the blood of their victims like the Vampires did, but they didn't stop there. They drained their victims dry and then would feast on the flesh and organs. They would break their victim's bones open and suck out the marrow. A human in their grasp would be plucked clean in an *hour*. And no matter how much they ate, they were always hungry.

The one he was tracking had managed to filch a young woman who had been walking in the gardens that surrounded the base of the Spire. Tarn had found what remained of her–just a long slender arm, the color of alabaster–and brought it to him. He had recognized the scent of decay that the Hags always left behind. He'd dipped the tip of Borage into one of the gnawed portions of the arm to give it a taste of the Hag. And then they'd gone on the hunt.

Caemorn loved to wander far into the seemingly endless woods that surround Solace. Because no sun ever shone here, there was no clock in the back of his mind telling him he must find shelter. He could just go on and on, sleeping wherever he wished, often in the boughs of the huge trees.

Despite living in Solace for over ten thousand years, the whole world had not been seen. In fact, only a small portion of it had been. The truth was it was too dangerous. Once out of the view of the city, the Ever Dark was wild, utterly untamed. Creatures far more fear-some than the Night Hags moved under the thick canopy of trees or swam in the seemingly endless black and silver oceans, or hid beneath the sands of deserts so vast that they could have swallowed the Sahara whole.

Many Vampire explorers had set out to see if they could reach the other Vampire cities in the Ever Dark, to prove or disprove the hypothesis that each city was its own pocket universe that didn't touch one another, but none of them ever saw the entirety of the planet. Most never came back. And those that did, those that had gone *far*, when they returned were different. They spoke only in whispers of what they'd seen, whispered words that made no sense.

When Caemorn had hired a powerful Eyros Vampire to search the mind of one of these explorers, both Vampires had gone mad and had to be put down. Such a thing was never attempted again. Even trying to interrogate the soul of this explorer had led many a Kaly Vampire to retreat to her tower room and never come out.

Most of these explorer Vampires would just leave the confines of the city and disappear into the woods, never to be seen or heard of again. Whether they went back to whatever terrible wonder they had found out there that had taken their minds or whether they simply experienced their Second Deaths, no one knew.

But while these stories frightened most Vampires into staying close to the cities, or even retreating to Earth, for Caemorn, the unknown vastness called to him. He sometimes thought he should have been one of those explorers. He would not be taken by whatever the others had found that had driven them mad. A Kaly Vampire must look into the mouth of madness, the eyes of death, and not look away. They must survive such an encounter not once, but countless times. Only those strong enough to do this survived.

But his Master Artemis Alucius had determined from the moment he was made that he was for the Order. He would be the one Kaly to become so trusted and revered that he would bring all their Bloodline up in esteem. And he had done it, but the esteem that his Master craved didn't exactly become theirs. No matter what the Kaly Vampires did, they were distrusted, because they dabbled in *death* and Vampires feared death far more than mortals did. So the Kalys were considered tainted in some way.

Even now, Caemorn knew that there were many out there who would have preferred a new Preceptor, in fact, would have preferred the exiled Arcius Kane. His grin turned to a grimace. He would never give up his role as Preceptor. They would have to take it from him and few were powerful enough to even try. But that also meant, he could not give in to the call of the vastness, could not become the greatest explorer of Vampire kind. No, he would remain chained to Solace's Spire.

Caemorn adjusted in the fine, tooled saddle. His crimson and black silk cloak billowed out behind him like a pair of wings as Neboa cantered through the woods. His armor–black as well with red etchings of skulls and vines on the front and back–sat comfortably on his muscular frame.

This armor, too, was found in the armory. When not worn, it was a five inch by five inch metallic disk. If one slapped that disk against one's chest, the armor *grew* from it and completely engulfed the Vampire's form, no matter what the Vampire's dimensions. The armor was impervious to gunfire and blades. Only other magical weapons appeared capable of harming it, at least so far as they knew. Again, it seemed strange to him that neither Seeyr nor her people had used such amazing pieces to defend themselves.

Perhaps they could foresee it was pointless. That no matter what they did, they would lose. So why bother trying?

He could not imagine simply giving up. He would fight to the last breath of his Second Life. But if one could see their own death, over and over again, would one still be able to fight? Or would it be as if one had died already?

Death for a Kaly both held no fear and was terrifying at the same time. They knew what the spirit could be used for. He used the power of souls to fuel his magic, to do his will. There was nothing more terrifying than the thought of a Kaly's own soul used in such a manner. He knew that there would be an eternity of pain and torment ahead of him if that was the case. So that was where the fear lay. But the Kaly knew that the soul did go on and some actually glimpsed that next world so that was why they did not fear their Second Deaths.   Maybe the Seeyr Vampires saw that place, too.

He had never asked Seeyr this. In truth, he loathed being in her presence. He always had this feeling that she was mocking him though she had never been anything but respectful. He feared that she simply reflected back his own uncertainties about himself. Just as he wore this armor, he wore his Master's desires for him just the same. Only Artemis, outside of Fiona, knew about Nightvallen being discovered. That was part of the reason he was out of the Spire and hunting.

"You've sent Confessor Darksilver to investigate? Are you sure that's wise?" Artemis had asked him through the Glass.

Every city had at least one Glass, many had far more. They were the Skypes of Ever Dark, allowing one to speak and see another person between the cities. They looked like mirrors except they did not reflect anything, but instead showed boiling clouds of gray smoke until it connected to another Glass.

"Fiona has a brilliant tactical mind and she keeps secrets well," Caemorn had tried to resist his voice from tightening at the criticism. Even though he was over 1400 years old and Preceptor, Artemis still treated him as if he were the newest of fledglings. Perhaps compared to the 5000 year old Kaly Vampire he was.

Artemis looked nothing like his age. He had been turned at nearly the first bloom of youth at only fifteen. He had curly blond hair that fell across a pale, unlined brow and large silver eyes that seemed to fill his heart-shaped face. He was fine boned and slender like a reed. He often wore a simple white tunic with a gold belt and a wreath of green leaves atop his head rather like a young Cupid. That was the outfit he had on now as he lounged on a sofa of fine blue silk. Everything about Artemis gave the impression of softness and innocence. But he was neither soft nor innocent.

Though turned before he reached full manhood, Artemis had founded his own House only a few hundred years into his life. In the Kaly Bloodline where there were only two dozen Houses, as few fledglings survived the brutal training, it was unheard of for such a young Vampire to do as Artemis had. But Artemis had defied all the odds and carved a place for himself in the Kaly empire. He ruled the city of Lasting, though there were many older Vampires that wanted that spot. But Artemis kept them at bay with seeming ease.

"Fiona Darksilver is still devastated at the loss of her mentor, Arcius Kane," Artemis said testily. He pointed at Caemorn's chest. "You know this. That's why you sent her to spy on House Ravenscroft."

"You make it sound as if I intended to test her and not discover what he and Balthazar know," he answered coolly.

"Didn't you?" Artemis tugged on a blond curl. "I understand that Arcius is your particular *bug bear*, Caemorn. He is everything you are *not*, including beloved of the people."

Caemorn dug his fingernails into his palms, but did not allow the sharp pain he felt to be reflected on his face. "I sent her, because she is intelligent and knows Arcius well. Whatever affection she has towards him, he surely has *more* towards her. He will reveal to her–"

"I highly doubt he will reveal *anything*." Those large silver eyes pinned him in place. "Arcius may appear to be a friendly bear, but he is still a bear. He will eat you if you get too close. I do not know why people automatically associate friendliness with safety. Those who we perceive as friendly get to approach while others do not. Easier to strike from a closer position."

Caemorn felt fileted under his Master's dissection of his actions, but he continued to remain calm as he explained, "No vessel is perfect. Fiona is loyal to the Order. She is very pious. I balanced that against her relationship with Arcius. It was the best choice."

Artemis regarded him silently, one hand twirling a lock of that pure gold hair. "Yes, I can see that you attempted to act for the best. But this whole situation feels like we are riding a knife's edge, Caemorn. Fail, and you do more than simply disappoint me."

Not that disappointing Artemis wasn't extremely dangerous in and of itself. But that remains

"I realize that," Caemorn answered, but found that his mouth kept moving, "Perhaps it was unwise for you to insist that I kill the Harrows."

Artemis went very still and looked more like one of those Greek statues he seemed to pattern himself after. "Oh?"

Caemorn licked dry lips, but now that he had said it, he might as well go on with it. "Without his parent's deaths, Julian Harrow would never have become Hell bent on discovering our existence."

"And you think the Harrows themselves would have let go of this rabbit after they had found Nightvallen?" Artemis' tone was almost curious, as if he were considering what Caemorn was saying.

"We could have made them forget. With the assistance of an Eyros—"

"There is only *one* Eyros Vampire that could have ensured that people of the Harrows' mental strength never remembered and did not go mad or simple from the process. And, as I recall, you were not willing to ask for his help," Artemis reminded him, the curious tone becoming cutting in an instant.

Balthazar. It always comes back to him and his blasted exiled House!

"He would have demanded readmittance to the Ever Dark. We could not do that and to have him know about Nightvallen's existence—"

"But I am betting he does know about it now. If the rumors are to be believed, Julian is Daemon's fledgling and Christian is his." Artemis shook his head and his golden curls bounced becomingly. He almost looked cute. Caemorn wished he could rip those locks off.

"We'll know more when Fiona reports in," he answered neutrally. He refused to believe anything until he heard it directly from her.

"I expect to hear from you as soon as that happens," Artemis said sternly.

"Of course."

The Glass had gone dark as the connection was cut. Caemorn's shoulders slumped as the tension drained out of him. Artemis was not faithful. He had never believed in the godliness of any of the Immortals. He had never believed that Daemon had saved the Vampires from the Immortals' deprivations during the War. In fact, he believed that everything they thought about the Immortals was false. After all, if they were so powerful how could they keep Seeyr locked up for so long? He had repeatedly pointed out to Caemorn that Daemon's alleged special power, Armageddon, was simply made up.

"The word *Armageddon* is a Hebrew word associated with the second coming of Christ. Daemon was long asleep when the human's Jesus allegedly walked the Earth," Artemis had said with a dismissive wave of his hand.

"Perhaps the name is simply new, but the power is old," Caemorn had suggested.

But Artemis had dismissed that possibility. "Even if what you are saying is true then the Vampires who would have seen it would not have likely been old enough to have seen Daemon use it. There are none of our kind still existing from that age. None that aren't mad as hatters."

Yet Caemorn knew that most Vampires wouldn't take that critical view of Daemon that Artemis had. Most were young and impressionable. They had been filled from the beginning of their Second Lives with the stories of Daemon saving them. The Order had made sure of that. Yet an actual Daemon, one that wasn't controlled by the Order itself, could destroy everything they had built.

And who knew what he would be like. Those who had lived through the War said nothing good about the Immortals and Daemon had led them before he went to sleep. Seeyr was frightening herself and strange beyond strange. Yet if the populace knew that Daemon was alive, awake, and ready to return? Unless the Order stopped him before that happened, they would have to *welcome* him back, even if that meant destruction in the long run.

Caemorn had begun to pace as he thought of all the terrible possibilities that could await them all in the future where the Vampire King roamed the worlds. If only he knew if that king now moved.

In some ways, things were far better on Earth, at least in terms of communication. He would have been able to call Fiona and hear from her immediately. But instead as he was in the Ever Dark he would have to wait for her to return. So he was grateful when Tarn had brought him the arm.

A hunt would clear his mind. It would give him something physical to do instead of simply waiting for news. He had ignored the slight tingle at the back of his mind as he had looked down at that perfect arm. The fact that it was *perfect*, other than the gnawing on the end bothered him. Normally, the Night Hag's draining of the blood would shrivel the flesh. Further, after eating the internal organs, the Hags normally feasted on the limbs first. Yet the hand and forearm were quite unmarked.

The pointer finger had been *crooked* as if to lure him in a certain direction. But he had been so anxious to move, he had ignored that faint warning feeling. He had Borage, Tarn and Farun, as well as his own powers. Few could challenge him alone, and certainly not when he had his beasts and magic weapon with him.

He tightened his hold on Borage and retracted his helmet. The Hag was heading towards a swampy, cleared area. He had been there before. He believed that the swamps were the Hag's natural habitats. Retreating to her lair there made sense, but something felt off.

He took in a deep breath. The clean air of the forest, scented with pine and snow, had changed to the richer, loamier scent of the swamp. The faint traces of sulfur and rot drifted over to him as well. His nose wrinkled. The swamp - though it could be alluring with the many drifting balls of blue fire that rose from the bubbling surface - wasn't his favorite place. Farun drew in a breath, too, and sneezed. The werewolf rubbed his nose in disgust. He didn't like the scent either.

Caemorn slowed Neboa to a walk as they approached the thinning treeline that marked the beginning of the swamp. He could already see the glowing orbs of blue fire rising from the swamp's murky surface. And right at the edge of those black waters stood a single Night Hag. It was the one that he had been trailing. She nibbled on the woman's other hand.

Tarn let out a curious grunt and Caemorn glanced down at him. That furry face showed confusion. The Hag should be running. But she stood there as if waiting for them. Convinced this was a trap, but feeling the undeniable urge to continue on, Caemorn slid off of Neboa's back and urged the horse to stay where she was. He and the werewolves strode towards the Hag.

The wet earth sucked at his boots, wanting to pull him down into its sticky embrace. The werewolves' fur up to their ankles was soon heavy with the stinking black mud. Caemorn's mood dampened with every sucking step. Finally, he stood a few feet from her. Borage glowed almost blindingly.

"You seek death?" he asked her.

The Hags could speak English, amazingly enough. They had likely heard the Vampires speaking it and seemed to have a rudimentary understanding of the language. The fact that they might be intelligent though did not stop him from killing them with ease.

This Hag took another bite from the woman's arm in response, chewing almost thoughtfully. Caemorn gritted his teeth. His fangs extended with his anger. This bitch had made him walk through mud. The werewolves would have to be thoroughly bathed and they hated the water. She'd taken one of his humans. He was not amused. Did she dare defy him as everyone else seemed to be doing lately?

"You shall have it then," he said and thrust Borage into her chest.

She let out a guttural sound and finally dropped the hand she was still nibbling on. But then she grasped hold of Borage and *pulled* herself up its length until she was nearly face to face with him. Her eyes, which had been pitch black, suddenly started to glow *red*. He flinched back before forcing himself to draw nearer.

She croaked out, her breath foul with rot, the following words, "The king... the king... the king has returned!"

Unnerved, more than afraid, Caemorn hissed, "Well, he won't be saving you!"

With a yell of rage, Caemorn tore off the Hag's head. His yell echoed throughout the swamp and the whirr of the night insects went silent at it. The blue orbs of fire did not even rise from the swamp's depths for a long moment. Farun, who had been sniffing the Hag's corpse, considering eating it, stilled suddenly. His shaggy head jerked up as did his brother's. They were staring out into the swamp that was suddenly lit up by the orbs once more.

Except they were not blue anymore. They were *red*.

151

DENIAL

"*N*o." Balthazar made a swiping motion through the air. "No. No. No. No. No. I am *not... not...* that person!"

Daemon lifted an eyebrow. The Vampire Lord was upset at the revelation that he was Eyros. He searched Balthazar's mind and it became immediately clear why that was. Daemon was amused, because it was such an *Eyros* thing to think.

"It goes against your view of yourself as the rebel, I take it? Not an outsider, but the ultimate insider?" Daemon asked.

Balthazar glanced around almost furtively, which amused Daemon more. All of House Ravenscroft was on a high from the oneness and didn't notice their leader's surreptitious actions, except for Christian and Julian. Those two were always hyper aware of him and Balthazar, because they were their Masters. Both fledglings crowded in nearer to hear, all wide-eyed and open-eared.

Balthazar leaned towards Daemon and hissed, "You do realize that Immortals are about as popular as the plague, right?"

Daemon spread his hands towards the chattering Vampires. "They do not think this."

Balthazar continued in a low voice, "That's only because you're *you*. Don't you know the stories? Hasn't Arcius told you our history? King Daemon is a *hero*. The rest of the Immortals? Not so much."

"What am I supposed to have told our king?" Arcius' eyes were bright with the oneness. He clapped a companionable hand on Balthazar's shoulder as he joined their smaller circle. "What's going on?"

"Haven't you told him about how the other *precious* Immortals are considered oppressors and enemies because of the War?" Balthazar demanded. "That Vampires celebrate their deaths? That everything Vampires stand for is in opposition to them?"

Arcius looked thoughtful. "The stories are simplistic, Balthazar. I can tell our king what is in the texts, but, as we all know, the victors write the books. A truly historic record... Well, those are suppressed by the Order."

"The more I hear about this Order, the more I don't like it." Julian crossed his arms over his chest.

"Do not judge us by Caemorn and the ignorant. Or try not to." Arcius scrubbed a hand over the back of his neck.

"Religious orders are known for dumbing things down. The simpler the tale, the easier it is to transmit and remember. And, in the past, not knowing how to read was common, though that's likely not as true of Vampires as the general population," Christian said with crisp precision. "I'm sure that nothing in this Order's history is likely accurate."

"It is not so bad as all that." Arcius though looked disturbed. Daemon sensed it was because he was now real to the Confessor and that changed things. "We were right about King Daemon, but as to the others—"

"So now you're saying that you *don't* believe in the very premise of the Order?" A sort of desperate anger was in Balthazar's eyes. "You don't believe that the Immortals deserved to die?"

"I believe that there is greatness in those that came before us, but weakness, too," Arcius said thoughtfully. "But I have never espoused the position that all Immortals were our enemies. Seeyr, for instance, tried to be neutral."

"And fat lot that did her and her fledglings! Her city in Ever Dark is overrun by the Order and her people cast aside to wander alone," Balthazar snapped. His gaze flickered to Daemon and then back to Arcius as he asked the Confessor, "What about Eyros? What does the Order say about him?"

Arcius' forehead furrowed. "What is this all about, Balthazar? You know the story as well as I do. Roan told it often enough of how he was one of the ones to overthrow Eyros' yoke of oppression."

"What was the story exactly? How did Eyros die? I assume he died, didn't he?" Christian asked.

Balthazar's hands were on his hips and he said tightly, "Eyros attempted to stop the War by trying to take over everyone's minds and control them all. He would *make* them want peace."

"It is said that he did so in order to calm things down. He wanted to stop the killing and re-establish order," Arcius said almost gently. "You make it seem like he wanted to simply control everyone for his own gain."

"Of course he did!" Balthazar pressed his lips together as he noticed people turning their heads to see why his voice was raised. Keeping his voice low, he added, "Maybe there was some good intent behind it, but, come on, think about it! He wanted to be king." Balthazar's gaze flickered up to Daemon again and he said, almost bitterly, "But he *wasn't* king. He wasn't anywhere near strong enough to succeed. And by trying to control everyone, he stretched himself too thin. Exhausted himself. And then all of them came after him. They ripped him apart. Roan bragged that he had a piece of Eyros' skin. Remember he'd stitched that thing into one of his cloaks? I burned that goddamned thing, but I still remember his caressing it!"

Both Julian and Christian looked horrified at what had happened to Eyros. Daemon's mood darkened as well. Eyros had been one of the closest of the Immortals to him. To think that he had been ripped apart by the Vampires–their children–was unthinkable! But he put that aside as his disbelief would not help Balthazar accept who he truly was. His whole view of Eyros was skewed.

"If you fear that Eyros was simply an opportunist, Balthazar, let me put your mind at ease," Daemon told them. He cast his mind back to his friend with the wild, hedonistic personality. "Eyros was quite idealistic in a way. He had confidence–some would call it arrogance, at times–in his ability to persuade. And I could very well see him trying to do as you suggest, to take control, to pull people back to reason. But he wouldn't have done it to be king. He never wanted that kind of power. Oh, he wanted to be in the throne's *reflected* light, but that was all."

Balthazar listened intently to him. Some tension seemed to bleed out of him, but not altogether. "Eyros was still ripped apart. The Vampires must have had reason to do what they did."

"Have you ever been in a war, Balthazar?" Daemon asked carefully. "Because I assure you that logic and reason often play no part in it. At least, not on the battlefield."

"So you're saying that Eyros is not a complete rat bastard?" Balthazar's voice was brittle, but hopeful.

Arcius cast a strange look at Balthazar, clearly not understanding what was going on with his reactions, but then he turned towards Daemon. "That is good to know, King Daemon Though we take pride in our mind control abilities, we are often seen as–"

"Scum," Balthazar interjected. "We're thought of as untrustworthy in Vampire society. Eyros' name is used as a curse word. We act like it's a badge of honor, but if anyone were to actually see Eyros return… if he were to be truly reborn…"

Arcius' forehead furrowed deeper. "Is Eyros still alive, Daemon? Do you sense him? Were the stories of his terrible death untrue? Is that what the two of you are talking about?"

Daemon and Balthazar locked gazes. There was a pleading look in those angry silver eyes that stared into his. *Please don't tell.* That was Balthazar's request.

Oh, old friend, I will give you time to come to terms with this, Daemon thought. *But lying to Arcius is not what you should be doing. Of anyone, Arcius would understand and still love you.*

"No, I am not suggesting that at all, Arcius." And Daemon wasn't. But what he was saying was far more profound. Eyros had died. Eyros had been reborn. Balthazar was Eyros.

But it is the truth and he must accept it eventually.

Balthazar's shoulders slumped as if he were a popped balloon. He ran a hand through his hair. "Thank you–thank you for the gift of the oneness, Daemon. It is very useful, I'm sure."

He also meant thanks for keeping his secret.

"You will see the benefits of it in the coming days, weeks, months, years and beyond," Daemon answered solemnly.

Because you are Eyros and the oneness will reach beyond this single House of Vampires and stretch to every member of your Bloodline, Daemon thought, but did not say. *But you are not ready to know this yet.*

Christian put a hand on Balthazar's slightly bowed back, which immediately had the Vampire Lord perking up and smiling at his fledgling.

"We are not responsible for those who came before us, Balthazar," Christian said quietly, believing that this was what was concerning Balthazar. "We just have ourselves to contend with."

Balthazar paled. That was clearly what he was afraid of: himself. But he forced a thin grin on his face and responded, "You're right, of course, Christian." He turned to Daemon. "Are you certain, Daemon, that it is safe for my people to leave the compound tonight?"

"Yes. Fiona and the other Vampires fled. The Order must keep my existence a secret so they will not act openly against us. I would think going out this evening would be the safest time as they will not have had a chance to organize themselves after Fiona's failure. In fact, I am planning to take Julian out hunting myself. Do you have somewhere to be, Balthazar?" Daemon asked.

"I have to go to the House Margolies' Blood Den to review some of their candidates for Acolytes and I need to start looking for more suitable candidates for our own House as you have quite the appetite," Balthazar explained. "Not to mention that the other House members should go out and feed as well to let our Acolytes recover fully."

Daemon bowed his head. "I apologize for stretching your resources so thin. I am used to Houses having hundreds of Acolytes. Clearly, I allowed my assumptions to cloud my thinking."

He saw Arcius frowning at Balthazar. The Vampire Lord looked rather guilty in response.

"Daemon, I did not mean to suggest that you were not welcome to do as you did. I just wish our House to be more prepared to host you properly," Balthazar quickly amended, which had the frown leaving Arcius' face. "I truly mean this. I sometimes speak before I think. I am *happy* to host you, truly. I want you to consider this your home."

Balthazar's face showed both earnestness and a sort of confusion as the words were leaving his mouth. These feelings stemmed from deep within him. Daemon guessed that more of Eyros had awoken after the oneness. Balthazar would start to remember their friendship.

"I am honored." Daemon bowed again, which seemed to confuse Balthazar even more.

To offer one's House as a home for the king was a far bigger deal than Balthazar guessed, but Daemon would take it at face value. It meant he could simply usurp control of the house from the lord who was its head and bring it under his full dominion. He wouldn't, however, do that to Balthazar. There was no need and this House had been through enough.

"We're going hunting?" Julian asked.

Julian had brightened instantly at the idea of learning something new, but there was a slight queasiness too in his fledgling's mind. He saw the quick glance between Julian and Arcius. He knew it was about something that had happened when he'd left Julian alone in the bedroom and gone to Commune. While he was glad that Arcius had assisted his fledgling, his upper lip curled back from his teeth slightly at them sharing a secret.

It will not be a secret long. I will insist on knowing it.

"Before you go out, Daemon," Arcius said, "Balthazar has ordered a tailor to come to take your measurements and she has also brought some off the rack clothing that suits this time period."

"Oh, great!" Julian enthused. "Yeah, the leather pants and wolf fur coat isn't exactly going to be *subtle* if we're really going out hunting."

Daemon raised an eyebrow. "My clothes are classics."

157

"You look like a Vampire King in them," Sophia chimed in. She had wandered over at some point in the conversation, making herself unobtrusive until now.

A very clever child.

"That is the point," he told her.

"That is the point *most* of the time." Julian laughed and ran a hand down the fur coat with affection. "But aren't we supposed to be unnoticed? Your good looks and red eyes are already going to have people wondering about you."

He cupped Julian's cheek. "You've forgotten the lesson I gave you about Vampires obscuring their presences already?"

The memory of following the three Vampires to the Blood Den appeared in Julian's mind and his young fledgling brightened. "Oh, right, but still you'll need some new clothes, yeah? You don't just want to wear one outfit forever?"

"You're thinking I'll start to smell." Daemon's lips pursed in displeasure.

Arcius flushed and looked down at the ground. Christian let out a cough that sounded suspiciously like a strangled laugh. Balthazar was looking at Julian like it was his funeral. Sophia tee hee'd. Only his fledgling could get away with such a bold statement.

Julian slipped an arm around Daemon's waist. "There's this tale about the emperor's new clothes where all his subjects were too afraid to tell him the truth that he had no clothes on."

"I thought this was about me getting *new* clothes," Daemon pointed out.

"The moral of the story is that the emperor was put in an embarrassing situation because the people around him wouldn't tell him the hard truths," Julian explained, not looking worried at all that he would have a bad reaction. "As your fledgling, I feel it is my duty to tell you the truth. Which means you need new clothes so you don't smell bad."

Daemon considered this, and then he nodded. "I agree. In the past, Eyros and Seeyr were my truth tellers. I will let you be one as well."

Balthazar stilled a little and stared at the ground overly long. Sophia's smile grew wider as she then extended a hand to him.

"The tailor has just arrived. The three of us can go see her together! I need some new clothes, too, and Lord Balthazar has so kindly agreed to buy some for me," she said, casting a loving glance at Balthazar, who had agreed to no such thing. Or, at least, he hadn't been asked, but if he had been, he'd likely have said yes.

For his part, the Vampire Lord gave her a dry smile. "Of course, Sophia, I am happy to take care of all your needs as our newest member of House Ravenscroft."

"You are so thoughtful! As always!" She beamed at him.

Arcius' bushy beard did not quite hide the laughing smile on his face at that exchange, but then he grew somber. "I am going to venture out myself. I still have contacts in the Order. Maybe I can find out how much is known or suspected about Daemon."

"You're hoping that Fiona hasn't gone back to the Spire, aren't you? That she's rabbitted, but she'll seek you out." Balthazar's expression was curious as he said this. It was a mixture of exasperation in his bunched eyebrows and affection for Arcius in the faint smile.

"If she does come to me that would be a good thing, Balthazar. She is devout. Whatever other loyalties she may have, having seen Daemon... Well, I think that she will be reachable," Arcius said.

Balthazar shook his head. "You need to be careful with her, Arcius. Don't let your fondness for her blind you to the fact that she's under Caemorn's thumb."

"She would never harm me." Arcius shook his shaggy head.

"I'd rather you not give her the chance. If she hasn't gone to Caemorn then perhaps it should be ensured that she *never* does," Balthazar said with a certain modicum of reluctance, but Daemon saw Eyros' cold, practical sense peeking through too.

Arcius reared back. "Balthazar, we cannot stoop to their level! If we strike first then we are in the wrong! Even if your cause is just, doing an evil act will taint it forever!"

Balthazar shook his head. "I'm worried about keeping us safe, Arcius. If you don't think the Order will murder us all–"

"There is no need to take any such action," Daemon smoothly

interjected. He felt Julian and Christian's anxiety rising at this talk of death and destruction. "When the Order comes, I will take care of it."

"Forgive me, Daemon, but as impressive as you are, you're one person," Balthazar pointed out. "Caemorn will send at least a dozen of his top Confessors out after you."

"A *dozen?*" Daemon attempted to decipher if the Vampire Lord was joking that this was some sort of threat to him.

"They're highly trained. They're deadly. They can take out armies," Balthazar explained.

Julian tightened his hold on him. "You're not fully powered up, Daemon. I think we need to be careful."

If twelve Vampires could truly be a threat to him then he would have to stop being king. But he did not say this. They would not believe him. He was beginning to understand how much of a myth he had become.

"We will be. But we must go hunt for me to recover my strength in any event. I would not have others go out for me," Daemon replied evenly. "We will be safe, Julian. Do not worry."

He felt Sophia's silver eyes on him and he knew that she was aware of his strength. But she gave him the faintest of nods. Seeing would be believing for these Vampires. They had heard words for so long that were not true that they wouldn't believe anything but actions.

"Perhaps we should all go together to hunt," Christian suggested. He was frowning deeply. He clearly did not want his best friend in any danger.

"There is no need for that, Christian," Daemon interjected. "Your Master has things he must do and I know he wants you with him."

"Can we stop at my house to get clothes for Christian and me?" Julian asked Daemon.

"Your home will be watched," Balthazar pointed out. "Clothes are hardly a priority. We can have new ones bought."

"But our cameras and computers are there, too." Julian's nostrils flared with anger at those who were keeping him from his home. "We have a business to run. We need to figure out what we're going to do

160

with that. And it's our home, damnit. Nobody is going to frighten us away from it."

"None will see us enter or leave, Balthazar. Do not worry about that." Daemon tucked a stray curl behind Julian's ear. "And you shall have your home back, Julian. I swear that."

Balthazar still looked unconvinced, but seeing as he wasn't going to get them to do otherwise, finally said, "All right. But *all* of you be careful. I'm going to have a confab with the House now. Sophia, you're excused from this. Please take care of Daemon and Julian with the tailor."

She bobbed her head and did a sort of curtsy, which had Balthazar smiling.

"Oh, and Julian, there will be cell phones available for you and Daemon before you go as well with everyone's numbers programmed in. Keep in contact," he instructed.

"Will do," Julian assured him.

Daemon did not know what these "cell phones" were, but he would let Julian have one if necessary. He knew he had much to learn already. He did not reel with the thought of all the knowledge he had to absorb, but reveled in it. It had been so long since there had been anything new for him to know. Now there was a whole world of things.

Sophia grasped one of his hands and one of Julian's hands and started to tug them towards the main house, saying, "I cannot *wait* to see what the tailor makes of you, King Daemon! She'll be so amazed at how pretty you are. The perfect specimen of a man!"

"An Immortal," he corrected her gently.

"She won't know that! She's human. Don't you think Daemon is perfect, Julian?" she asked his fledgling who was looking over his shoulder at Christian.

The two best friends had not had a chance to talk. The need to confer with one another spoke in both their glances.

"Later tonight you will get your chance to speak with Christian," Daemon assured him.

"Oh, you guys are so cute!" Sophia remarked as she, too, noticed the rather desperate glances between Julian and Christian. "More like brothers than just friends."

"We are something like that. And, thanks, Daemon. We need to debrief each other," Julian explained, looking relieved. "Things aren't fully real for us if we haven't discussed them together."

"Aw! That's so nice! I'm so glad I'll be that close with you, too, in the near future," she enthused.

Julian just gave a laugh. "That's good to know, Sophia. Maybe we should just get over the middle part and be best friends."

"I think that's a brilliant idea!" she agreed.

"Then I'll have to learn more about you," Julian said.

"I promise you'll know it all. Now march! We have clothes to pick out!" she giggled.

As the three of them went towards the main house, Daemon felt his fledgling mentally tune into him.

Julian asked telepathically, *Daemon, what was going on between you and Balthazar at the end of the oneness?*

Daemon already knew his fledgling would be displeased with his actions, but he had been surprised to find his good friend in the brash young Vampire Lord. So he simply related that to Julian, *Balthazar is Eyros reborn. During the oneness that part of him was triggered.*

His fledgling's eyes went huge. *What? Holy shit!*

Yes, that is a moderate way to describe his emotions. He is having an identity crisis, Daemon replied. *As you heard, he does not exactly see Eyros as a hero in the War.* Daemon disliked even considering this, but he added, *And perhaps he was not. Though I am certain it was with the best of intentions that he acted. With self-interest, too. But all-in-all, I am grieved at the thought that there was such a breach between Vampires and Immortals to lead to such a brutal death.*

You sprung all that information on Balthazar, didn't you? Just told him right out of the blue that he is an Immortal? His fledgling rubbed his forehead and gave him a dubious look.

I thought he would be pleased. I was pleased to know it. Daemon wasn't exactly defensive about how he'd handled it, but he knew that he could have done better. *Balthazar enjoys power and respect. He wants more of it. He thinks he deserves it. Knowing he's an Immortal—*

Balthazar draws a lot of his power from those that follow him, Julian pointed out. *Would all of them be happy to know he's an Immortal? You were always portrayed as on the Vampires' side. But Eyros was one of the oppressors or whatever.*

While you have a point, Daemon conceded. *He is who he is, Julian. And he will have to deal with that at some time as he awakens to the fullness of his power.*

Julian's eyes narrowed. *What does that mean exactly? And did you tell him this fullness was coming?*

Daemon pursed his lips and tried not to look guilty. *I did not have a chance.*

Daemon! Julian sounded outraged.

There is still time to tell him yet. Just not tonight. He has had enough to take in this evening, Daemon told him.

But you will tell him, right? You'll prepare him for it? Julian carefully studied his face.

I will.

At that moment, they had passed into the main house and through it to a parlor. A woman with dark hair in two braids on either side of a hawk-like face had just come through the front doors. She took in Daemon in one head to toe glance. Her thick black eyebrows arched up.

"I see that I will be dressing a god tonight," she said, her voice deep and almost masculine.

Shit, I should have had you put on pants! Julian put a hand on his forehead in embarrassment.

On the contrary, I think this tailor understands her job perfectly well. Daemon grinned. *Let us be clothed in new garments and go out into the night.*

THE POWER OF REVENGE

⁂

*J*ulian hid a smile as Daemon modeled the clothes he intended to wear that night. Tailored black slacks that skimmed his long, muscular legs. A black button-down shirt, open at the throat, with silver and onyx cufflinks at his surprisingly elegant wrists. Dress shoes with a high polished shine. And filling it all out were his dark curling hair and sculpted good looks. He was rather breathtaking and Julian wished they were staying *in* rather than going *out*.

The smile came from the fact that Daemon was quite insistent that all his clothes be black or white. There could be some crimson highlights, such as an inner lining to a classic suit coat or embroidery on the cuffs and collar. But most colors were verboten. It reminded Julian of his impression of Ever Dark as a whole: all velvety blacks and ghostly whites with pops of color.

The tailor—whose name was Manx, just Manx, no last name—circled Daemon with a critical eye. Her right hand stroked her chin as her shoes tapped, tapped, tapped on the marble floor. Julian thought he felt a slight unease from the Vampire King about whether or not she would approve of how he filled out the clothes she had brought him.

She stopped in front of Daemon. She ran her hands unabashedly down his sides and tugged at the shirt to make it sit just so. "While I would like to tailor this further–it is a little too wide for those slim hips of yours–my understanding is that you need clothing to go out this evening in, yes?"

"Yes," Daemon agreed almost meekly.

"Then I shall *allow* you to wear this outfit tonight. When you are done with it, however, it should be returned to me for laundering and adjustment." Manx nodded at the end of her own statement as if this was bound to be agreeable to Daemon.

"Of course." More meekness from Daemon that Julian was going to love teasing him about later.

Manx was just a human after all. There was no royal blood in her veins. But she was the ruler here.

"Good," she said crisply.

Her head snapped towards Julian, who found himself standing up straighter. He slouched, according to her, hiding his good height. Again, with a critical eye, she approached him. She had brought him several off-the-rack items, too. He was wearing a pair of sinfully soft jeans that felt like he could just live in them forever and a white button-down shirt with a tan vest and matching shoes. She pulled on the vest and smoothed her hands over his shoulders.

"You are easier to dress than he is. Not so tall. Not so broad." Just when Julian was starting to get a tad of a complex for not being too much of anything–though compared against Daemon, who was? --he was rewarded by Manx with a, "You're just right. But still, everything can use a little tailoring. You, too, will turn this outfit over to me after the night is through, excluding the jeans. They are perfect."

Julian rubbed his hands over the fronts of the jeans. "They totally are."

"She has gotten you out of the potato sacks you usually wear," Daemon remarked as he looked Julian up and down.

"I don't wear potato sacks! Cargo pants and Henleys with utility vests are just *practical* for adventuring. Being dressed in wolf skins is not exactly a good wardrobe choice for tomb raiding," Julian protested.

He loved his cargo pants and Henleys. He was going to take a suitcase of them with him back here. Not even Daemon's disapproval would dim his adoration of them.

Daemon raised an eyebrow. "We will see. Come, we need to go to your home and then hunting. Where are the horses? I do not smell or hear any nearby." A frown had come to cross his lips.

Julian let out a soft laugh. Sophia chuckled, too. She had been sitting on a nearby couch, watching the two of them get measured and dressed. She'd offered to wait for her turn under Manx's critical eye until they were done since they had places to go while she intended to be lazy in her room. Julian was pretty sure that she wasn't really going to be lazy. Maybe she was going to look into the future or something. But he had a feeling that whatever she did would be useful.

"We don't have horses, Daemon," Julian explained, realizing then how a simple trip to his house *sans* other Vampires trying to kill them would still be an adventure or even an ordeal. Daemon had to learn everything and Julian had to somehow explain it in a way that made sense. "I mean we do, but we only really ride them for fun or sport. We use cars to get around. I'm sure that Balthazar has a car we can use or maybe we should call an Uber."

Julian spied the cell phones that Balthazar had mentioned sitting in a dish near the front door. Also in the dish were two sets of door keys likely for the house and a key fob. The key fob was to a Tesla. Julian grinned.

He threw one pair of the house keys to Daemon and a cell phone. The Vampire King caught them easily. He stared at both for long moments, twisting them in his hands. When the phone lit up, he jerked it away from his face with a growl. Julian and Sophia exchanged an amused glance.

"You're going to have so much fun showing him the world, Julian!" Sophia sauntered over to him as she said this. Leaning against his side, she added, "He'll be like a child again. All wonder and awe. It's good for him. Life before had gotten so stale."

Julian put an arm around her slender shoulders, surprised at how close to her he already felt. Though she was far older than him, she was the exact sort of little sister he would have wanted. He was pretty sure of the answer to this question, but he wanted to confirm, "You weren't around when he was, were you?"

"Oh, no! I'm nowhere near that old." She waved a hand. "But Seeyr told me all about him. She missed him so."

"Well, he's back now and we'll find Seeyr, too." He hoped they would. But the question was: would Seeyr still be herself or would she have been reborn like Eyros was?

The two of them regarded Daemon as he tapped the phone, causing the light to go on and off, in a fascinated fashion. He actually sniffed it at one point and his nose wrinkled. Knowing what a badass Daemon actually was made this cat-like curiosity even more adorable.

"Sophia!" Manx waved for the child-like Vampire to join her. "We must get started with your measurements."

Julian squeezed her to him for a moment more before releasing his grip on her. She took a few steps away.

She called over her shoulder, "Have fun! I know you will!"

She then skipped to Manx. Julian tensed a little though. Was she saying that because she truly foresaw them having fun that night? Or when she mentioned "fun" did she mean danger and adventure? Or...

He shook himself. He couldn't worry about the future. It would come as it would come. He had enough to worry about in the present, which included getting Daemon into a car and not having him get freaked out by the experience of a motor, lights, and moving really fast.

Julian went over to the Vampire King and slid an arm around his waist. He was amazed at how easy it was to touch Daemon now. There was an almost tactile need in him to touch the Vampire King. He had never been clingy around boyfriends before–he wasn't even sure they *were* boyfriends–so this need worried him slightly.

I'm worried that I'm comfortable around him? This is insane.

"What is insane?" Daemon lowered the phone.

"That we're standing around here when there's a beautiful night out there ready for us to discover," Julian half-lied.

Daemon nodded. With one last fascinated glance at the slim phone, he slipped it and the keys into the pockets of his tailored trousers. The two of them walked out of the house together. A Tesla, snow white and sleek, was parked on the curving front drive. The car lit up when Julian pressed the unlock button. Daemon reared back much like he had done with the phone.

"What is–is *that?*" Daemon hissed as he stared at the Tesla like it might bite him.

"That is a car. It is transportation instead of a horse. Come on. Let me show you how it works."

Julian linked his hand with Daemon's and pulled the Vampire King over to the vehicle. He opened the front passenger door and gestured for Daemon to get inside.

The Vampire King did not move. He stared at the plush leather interior with continuing distrust. His eyes seemed to measure the space inside and found it wanting despite its quite gracious dimensions and considerable legroom. Daemon straightened.

"No," he said softly.

"Uhm, what?"

"No, we are not getting into that coffin. I have had *enough* of small spaces." Daemon took two steps back.

Any inclination that Julian had to cajole him inside died with that last line. He hadn't considered that Daemon might be traumatized from the years–centuries? Millennia?--trapped in the tomb. So he shut the door and relocked the car.

"I'm sorry," he said. "I didn't even think of that. We can walk. It's only a few miles."

Daemon's nostrils were flared and faint tremors were running through him. Julian reached over and ran his hands up and down Daemon's arms until the tremors stopped. The Vampire King did not look at him, rather stared off into the distance, clearly remembering something unpleasant.

When Daemon spoke though, it wasn't about the car or being trapped in that magical sarcophagus, it was about Julian. "I shouldn't have left you alone earlier."

Julian blinked. His freak out with the blood and Arcius seemed like ages ago already. He was sure that he would have more moments when being a Vampire became more *real* to him than maybe he would like it to be, but at the moment, he felt quite good and calm.

"It's okay. I'm fine now and–"

"You do not understand." Daemon focused on his face then. "You are the one I have been waiting for and I–I was not there when you needed me."

Julian considered this. Would it have been better if Daemon had been there when he'd woken up? Yes and *no*. Arcius understood his freak out and could say the right things, because he'd once been human. Daemon had always lived with drinking blood, or so Julian thought. He didn't actually know. But if Daemon had had another life, a different life than being a Vampire, it was so long ago, he likely didn't remember it.

"Come on, let's walk," Julian suggested.

Julian put a hand on Daemon's lower back as he pulled out his phone with the other hand. He was about to tap in his address to find out the best way to return to Wingate, when he realized he *knew*. He could smell his home. It was the strangest thing. He smelled leather and books and hot electronics and the faintest remnants of his parents' scents. All of those smells wrapped together was *home* and he would be able to find it easily. He could almost visualize the route that he had to take. So he slipped the phone back into his pocket and started to lead the way.

Balthazar's mansion was on the outskirts of town, giving the Vampire Lord far more open land than Wingate had, which was situated in the university park area in the middle of the city. There were few streetlights and fewer people out near here unlike closer to the center. Julian was grateful for that, because he realized with a start, he was getting *hungry*.

"You are saying nothing, but you do not agree with me," Daemon said as they walked arm in arm down the street.

"I think that you can't and shouldn't be the only person I rely on," Julian finally said. "Arcius was there and he knew exactly what was going on and how to help me."

"And you think I would not have?" Daemon's voice was neutral but the toss of his head and slightly flared nostrils alerted Julian that he did not feel neutral about this.

"Daemon, you can't be jealous of Arcius." Julian tugged the Vampire King closer.

"I enjoy Arcius, but perhaps he is too familiar with you." Daemon sniffed.

"*Familiar*? You make it sound like I'm the son of a nobleman!" Julian stopped. "That *is* what you're saying, isn't it? Since I'm your fledgling that I'm like royal or something."

"You are royal. You are of my blood. You are the Vampire Prince."

While that had a charming, old-fashioned tone to it on the one hand, Julian bristled at it on the other.

"Arcius treats me just fine, I'll have you know! I wouldn't want him all bowing and scraping. He's totally respectful and kind to me. I don't want you saying anything to him about familiarity," Julian growled slightly. "This has got to do with you being jealous."

"You are quite *direct* with your wishes."

"Am I too *familiar* as well?"

That got him a smile and a shake of Daemon's head.

"Good. Because remember the emperor's new clothes? This is one of those moments," Julian reminded him. "Arcius is my friend. He is your Confessor. He practically worships the ground you walk on and that's good. But I don't want him to treat me like that. I'm not *you*."

Daemon was silent, but the stiff necked posture had left him. "Perhaps. I do appreciate Arcius. And I am glad he was there for you. But it should have been me that you relied upon. I will not forgive myself for that. I will be more assiduous in the future."

Julian suppressed a smile and a sigh. Those words had him picturing Daemon placing him in a tower shaped rather like a bird's cage and closing the door to keep him safe. Julian, of course, would be hammering at those bars in no time. So he said, "You're the king. You're going to have to do loads of things. You're not going to always be able to be here for me."

"You only think this because of how I treated you when I first turned you." Daemon's mouth was flattened and his forehead was bunched. "You think that you cannot trust me being there. By not being there tonight I just confirmed that."

"No! Okay, maybe a little but... no, at the same time." Julian stopped at an intersection.

The city was starting to come more alive. There was more traffic and more people on the streets. His senses were suddenly on fire. He was smelling cologne and exhaust, body odor and oil. He heard traffic, talking, dogs barking, heartbeats, the whoosh of blood in veins, and so much more. He curled himself closer to Daemon's body as if purely being closer to the Vampire King could shield him from his own heightened senses. He studiously tried to ignore everything and everyone else. It soothed him slightly.

"Of course, part of me wants you to always be there," Julian confessed as he sheltered in Daemon's larger than life presence. "And if you were the one saying that you wouldn't be, I'd be freaking out. I *love* that you're saying you want to be. I'm trying to be a good partner. I need you to know that I understand there might be times when you can't be there. That I'll figure it out on my own, if I have to and I'm okay with that."

Daemon smoothed his hands down the sides of Julian's head and kissed him gently. "Do you not know that you are the *most* important part of my existence? Julian, you are my *treasure*. You are what I will fight for. What I will protect with everything I am."

"Oh, that's... that's..."

Daemon didn't wait for any reply but just kissed him softly again. Tenderly. Reverently.

Julian blinked rapidly, fighting off unexpected emotions. That part

inside of him that had wailed like a lost child when he'd been separated from Daemon in the beginning clamped onto those words and
hugged them close. It was a part of himself that he wasn't altogether
sure he was comfortable with. It reminded him of how he'd been after
his parents' deaths.

He'd promised himself back then that he wouldn't cling to people,
that he would be all right even if stripped of everyone from his life.
That he wouldn't depend upon anyone. Except that hadn't really been
true. There had been Christian's parents and, of course, there had
been Christian himself. He would have died without his best friend a
million times over by now. But did he know Daemon enough to trust
him with that kind of importance in his life?

They started walking again. Neither spoke. Julian watched
Daemon with a growing fascination. Who was this being walking
alongside of him? On the one hand, Julian felt this complete harmony
being by Daemon. There was this sense that he could and should say
whatever was on his mind. He knew that Daemon was far older than
him–and, undoubtedly, far wiser–but Daemon still wanted to hear
Julian's thoughts and was open to even agreeing with them.

Daemon was also a predator. He'd seen that with Selene and Heath
in Nightvallen. The quick and easy way that Daemon had killed them,
the pleasure he'd seemed to take in doing that, was disturbing, but it
also drew Julian in. Would he ever kill his enemies with such eager
abandon? He couldn't quite imagine it, but then he sort of could, too.
With powers like Daemon's, wouldn't life feel a little more like a
videogame than reality?

Or maybe he should be drawing on the roles of superheroes and
following the "with great power comes great responsibility" line? He
wasn't sure. Other than the strange sensitivity to smells and sounds,
he felt normal, or rather a little peppier than normal. And he realized
at that moment, he could see just as well in the darkened yards as
what was under the golden pools of light created by the streetlamps.
Still, he didn't feel quite super powered yet.

"When are my powers going to kick in? And which ones will they
be?" he asked.

Daemon's eyebrows rose even as his lips twitched. "You are afraid of falling behind Christian?"

"Maybe a little. But he will only have Eyros' gift of mind control, right? But I will have more than one gift, because you have all of them?" Julian guessed.

He *hoped* he had at least one gift. He hoped that there wasn't a chance he could be a dud.

Daemon chuckled. "You've already started showing signs of having several of the gifts. But you've only fed once, Julian, and you've been a Vampire for less than two days."

"This is where you tell me to be patient and that I have all the time in the world—"

"You do." Daemon stroked the back of Julian's hand. "I am beginning to understand a little of your quickness. You rush forward."

"And I try to drag you with me." Julian grinned.

"You do. And while endless contemplation is not wise, quick action is not always wise either. So we are starting at level zero with you and moving from there." Daemon made a gesture in front of them.

"Level *zero*, huh?"

"Yes, and what does level zero tell you about our surroundings?" Daemon stopped in the middle of the sidewalk and people streamed around them.

There were no angry words said under people's breaths though he and Daemon were blocking their way. No one seemed to notice them at all. Julian realized that Daemon had cloaked them at some point and he hadn't noticed.

It was a good thing he had. Those red eyes of the Vampire King's would have caused people to stare as they glowed in the dark like fires, but no one even glanced their way. And there were far more people around them than he'd noticed before too. They were in the middle of town, just a block away from Wingate, following his nose and innate sense of direction. But he'd been so much in his head that he hadn't noticed where they actually were.

It's more than me just thinking hard. It's...

"You're shielding me," Julian realized, blinking as he thought about how when they'd stopped earlier he'd been bombarded with smells and sounds, but his senses were dampened down to almost normal now.

"Yes."

"You noticed I was having trouble and you... you just took care of it."

"Of course. I am your Master, Julian. It is my duty to take care of you," Daemon's answer was forthright and without any drama. As if this was normal and right and *ordinary*.

Julian was having a hard time processing this though. Christian took care of him in many ways and he tried to do the same for his best friend. But this kind of caring was unknown to him since his parents' deaths. Again, his eyes stung with tears that he refused to shed. It was ridiculous for him to be on the verge of crying twice in one night when he had not cried in *years*. His sensitive eyes caught sight of the tower on his house, on Wingate, the place he loved most in all the world. The place his parents had made a home for him and Christian. Seeing *home* brought more emotions swirling to the surface.

"I don't know how to..." Julian turned away from Daemon then. He needed to compose himself.

"You are not used to being cared for," Daemon murmured, more to himself than Julian, or so it seemed. "You have had to be so strong since..."

"Since my parents died." Julian's throat felt thick with emotions.

He hadn't really thought of his parents since he'd been turned. Now, their loss and the fact that he was the *same* as the beings who had killed them met in his head. He shuddered and swallowed hard.

Daemon stroked his back. Up and down. Down and up. Easing the terrible tension and anger that gripped him. There was bewilderment, too. He leaned over and put his hands on his thighs. He was having a hard time breathing.

"It is all right," Daemon said with quiet authority.

"It can't be. How can it be? I'm a *Vampire*. I'm the thing that–that *killed* them," he got out.

Daemon was silent for long moments. "Would you hate yourself for being human if human thieves or thugs had killed your parents?"

"No! But they were killed because they found out about Vampires existing and–"

"They could have found out any number of secrets that humans want to keep secret and been killed for those," Daemon gently pointed out. "But not all humans would be liable for what happened to them. Just like not all Vampires are. And *you*, surely are not. Nor are Balthazar or his group. I am actually rather certain that the one that hunts us now–this Caemorn Lorsus of the Order–is responsible."

Julian whipped around, shocked to know the villain of his story. Caemorn Losus. If he killed Julian's parents, there would be hell to pay.. "If he killed them... Can we get to him?"

"In time." Daemon stood tall and confident.

His expression though was not one of eagerness to go after an enemy, but patience. Julian's hands clenched at his sides. All those years of being able to do nothing to prove his parent's deaths were murders and not an accident burned inside of him and he seethed at Daemon's seeming indifference.

"But he's a threat!" Julian cried. "He wants to kill you and me both! Plus our friends! He's dangerous!"

"He's unimaginative," Daemon disagreed.

"*Unimaginative*? What? How does that matter? He still wants to hurt us and those we care about!"

"You've seen what Balthazar can do with his powers. How he wiped the Vampires' minds of all memories of you in the Blood Den. Such a thing could have easily been done to your parents with a simple command that they *avoid* all things Vampire forever more," Daemon pointed out. "But Caemorn didn't. So that tells me something about him. He sees everything as such a threat so he always overreacts. He thinks that this makes him look strong, but it reveals him as *weak*."

"My parents are still dead! He might be unimaginative and weak, but he has power! He killed my parents and no one cared! He didn't pay for it! There was no justice! There must be!"

"Yes, you are right. Forgive me." Daemon cupped his face. "But I was not there then. You were only a boy when it happened. You were only human. But not anymore. If you wish to think of your Vampire nature in any way in relation to your parents think of it like this: as a *benefit*. It will allow you to truly strike back at the person who took them from you."

Julian's face burned with emotion and tears leaked out. Angry and agony-filled. He realized then that he had not been dealing with these feelings about his parents or anything else since he'd been turned. Too much had been happening–most of it exciting and positive–for him to really *think* about his life now. But, here he was, having a breakdown and yet Daemon wasn't phased in the least. Maybe he had been wrong to think that Daemon wouldn't have known how to handle him in the bathroom that morning.

"I'm not alone in this. That's what you're saying? You're going to help? You won't let what happened to my parents just go because Caemorn is a Vampire, too?" Julian asked, more like demanded, to know.

"Who is this Caemorn to me? Nothing. Who are you to me? Everything. And if you worry that I am acting in a brash manner towards my subjects, Caemorn is exactly the *wrong* person I want running a religion or having any sort of power," Daemon answered.

"Yes, yes, exactly!"

"He could have acted far more prudently in regards to your parents, and I am sure about many other things. He has not. He has proven himself unworthy already, even if he hadn't harmed you and sought to harm me. Julian, this will be handled. You will have all the revenge you want," Daemon promised him. His thumbs glided down Julian's cheeks, soothing the heat that flamed in them. "Now breathe. Let go of this anger. At least some of it. For now. Reach for your joy in adventure."

Julian sucked in the cold, fall air and relished the feeling of it in his lungs. He continued doing this for long moments. His anger did recede. His lust for adventure had always been stronger. Daemon's soothing presence allowed the tension to bleed out of him, too. And it was during this relaxation that he sensed the other Vampires near his house. He stiffened again, but this time with alarm.

"Ah, I see you have noticed our *friends*. Fear not, they have no idea we are here," Daemon told him.

Julian's vision picked out two stealthy red-limned figures. One was hiding on the roof of Wingate while the other loitered in the back garden. But they weren't the only people coming to the house. Daemon started to frown as Julian stepped towards Wingate unconsciously. These two people's scents he would recognize anywhere. His hearing even flickered into their conversation.

"Just because neither of the boys has answered their cell phones, Liz, doesn't mean there's anything wrong," Henry Thorne, Christian's father, said with a touch of annoyance. But there was a little anxiety there, too, though he didn't want to acknowledge it.

"Christian and Julian *live* online, Henry. They're never away from their phones or computers longer than a few minutes. But I haven't gotten any response from them in two days," Liz Thorne, Christian's mother, answered.

He heard the tap of their shoes going up the front walk. The other Vampires did, too. And these Vampires started moving towards Christian's parents. Julian knew, without a doubt, that these Vampires intended to make Christian an orphan just like Caemorn had made him.

He was *not* going to let that happen.

TEACHABLE MOMENTS

*D*aemon knew that Julian was going to take off after the Vampires the moment that Christian's parents arrived. He could have gleaned who the couple were from Julian's mind, but simply the scent of them gave them away. They smelled of Christian's blood. Julian's terror on their behalf told him how beloved they were to his fledgling.

Christian's parents. Julian's practically adopted parents. Fragile. Mortal. Human.

He could have stopped Julian easily and gone after the Vampires that threatened the Thornes himself. Not even a breath would have had to be spared ordering Julian to remain where he was, and Julian would have stayed right there no matter how much he wanted to move. His power over his fledgling was *absolute*. Though he did not want Julian to know that. His fledgling must not fear him. And even if Julian wasn't afraid, the knowledge that Daemon could completely control him would cause his strong-willed fledgling to *chaff*.

And in this case, he must make his own decision and his own mistakes. Though I will not let the Thornes or Julian be harmed.

So he merely followed after Julian, to keep him and the Thornes safe, but also to see what his fledgling would do.

Julian had taken five long strides and leaped. With that single bound, Julian had left the sidewalk and flown across the street, above the wooden fence, and past the rose bushes. Julian had then landed silently in a half crouch on the closely cropped grass of his backyard. His fledgling had not even noticed this act of superhuman strength and speed, because he was so intent on what was happening in the front of the house.

Christian's mother smelled of wisteria and linen, while Christian's father smelled of leather and old paper. Their blood was rich and meaty. He knew that he would be refreshed from their veins, but they were not food. They were friends. Perhaps.

From Julian's mind he came to understand that both of them were professors at the university where Julian's own parents had taught. But the Thornes were not adventurers. They were very much people of the mind. But even the athletic and fearless Harrows would have been no match for even the newest of Vampires, so the Thornes had absolutely no chance against these Confessors, who were trained in the art of war.

But it is all relative. For these Confessors will be nothing against my fledgling, let alone against me.

Julian went for the one who had been in the backyard, but now was gliding around to the front. This Vampire–his name was Gerard, Daemon found out by skating over his mind–was thickly built with dark hair and stubble covering the jaw of his olive-skinned face. He moved with the oiled ease of a serpent. Daemon sensed the Helm Bloodline in Gerard.

Leave at least one of them alive, Julian, Daemon instructed. *We will need to question them.*

He felt an acknowledgement from his fledgling. He wondered if Julian would be able to control himself once the violence started. He did not wonder if Julian could take this 350-year-old Vampire. He *knew* Julian could.

Daemon stayed back at the end of the side path while Julian ranged forward on the balls of his feet. Gerard did not notice him coming until Julian was practically on top of him, even though

179

Daemon had released the glamour from around them the same moment they'd gotten into the yard. He would ensure that no humans saw them, but Julian had to deal with the Vampires on his own.

Gerard spun around just as Julian grabbed the back of his neck with one hand. Julian attempted to slam Gerard's head into the wall, but the Confessor shot a hand out to brace himself at the last moment and a *cracking* hit turned into only a glancing blow. Gerard then went *invisible*.

Julian became bewildered. He still had a hold on the back of Gerard's neck, but he could not see the Vampire he held. Julian suddenly curled forward, his mouth opening in an oomph as Gerard elbowed him.

Use your other senses, Julian. You are not relegated to only your eyes, Daemon advised. *Close them. Feel. Just feel. You will know everything you need to know. Believe.*

Julian hesitated, but then closed his eyes. Gerard tried to stagger Julian, but Julian aimed a wicked kick at the back of Gerard's left knee. There was a distinctive *snap*. Gerard did not scream even as his leg hung wrong. He clearly did not want to alert the Thornes of his presence.

But even wounded Gerard was a seasoned, skilled fighter. Julian was no slouch. His fledgling was a street fighter: doing what *worked* with an almost brutal efficiency over making any fancy moves. This likely came from Julian working in bad areas where he and Christian couldn't depend on the authorities to keep them safe.

Gerard tried to elbow Julian in the ribs again, but his fledgling twisted out of the way and rabbit-punched Gerard's side instead. All with his eyes *closed*. Another blow to Gerard's head. Another kick to the wounded knee that had Gerard down Gerard snarled silently and missed cutting Julian's legs out from underneath him.

You must end this soon, Julian. His partner is going to either go after the Thornes or come down here, Daemon let his fledgling know as he crossed his arms and leaned against the side of Julian's home.

Gerard must have realized that time was against Julian, too, and sent a desperate roundhouse that brushed against Julian's left cheek, but didn't land fully as Julian snapped his head to the side. A bruise formed, but would disappear once he fed.

Julian wrapped one arm around Gerard's neck and caught the Vampire in a sleeper hold. His fledgling's lips were skinned back. His fangs were out. A sleeper's hold could easily kill someone.

Listen to his heart, he advised Julian.

It was slowing. Gerard's eyelids slid shut. Julian released him. Gerard crumpled onto the ground. Julian though did not take even a second to congratulate himself. His head snapped up towards where the other Vampire–her name was Celeste–was about to drop down on top of the Thornes.

Jump. Do not think in human terms, Julian. You can reach the roof easily in one leap, Daemon instructed.

His fledgling flexed his legs and then rocketed upwards, making a parabolic arc to land on the roof by Celeste. Daemon floated to the roof to observe. It was then that the Thornes reached the front door.

"We should knock or ring the bell, Liz, not just go in," Henry said, a concerned lilt to his voice.

"Don't be silly. Julian gave us a set of keys for a reason. Besides, if they're not answering their phones or email then they will hardly be answering the door!" Liz responded. There was a rustling as she looked for the keys. "Damn, where are they?"

"Don't you have them on your key ring?"

"No, I put them in a special spot in my purse..."

Daemon turned back to Celeste. She had bone-white short hair and a wiry build. Though smaller than Julian, she was quick and agile. She'd danced away from him on the roof. Her expression showed a fox-like cunning. After taking out Gerard, Julian did not appear taxed. Instead, he was showing greater strength as the predator in him was aroused.

A brief glance into Celeste's mind told him that she knew Julian was a newly made Vampire by some Master who *claimed* to be Daemon. But everybody knew that couldn't be true. Daemon was a myth! Or, even if Daemon did exist, he was asleep somewhere far away. He hadn't made this Julian into a fledgling.

So she thought she could take Julian easily.

She darted in, racing across the roof's tiles on silent feet. Julian dropped down into a crouch, hands loose at his sides, and waited for her. Ten feet from him, she leaped. She wore spikes on her hands that were now extended. Julian dove out of her way. She slashed at him, but missed, he swept the legs out from under her. She stumbled but righted herself and spun back towards him, outrage on her face. Celeste sent a series of kicks at Julian's head. One. Two. Three! Julian leaped back and avoided each movement. He was a blur. Celeste's anger and bewilderment grew.

"Stay still!" she hissed.

"Try harder," Julian hissed right back.

And she did. Snap of her arm across the air that should have slapped him backwards. Stomping steps. Wicked kicks. Julian grabbed her right leg and tossed her. She regained her feet lightning quick. Her gaze fixed on Julian's.

"Who are you?" she asked.

"A Vampire. Just like you."

"No. You're not."

"You're right." Julian's eyes glowed red. "I'm the fledgling of the king."

"Can't be." She shook her head.

"I am."

She did not see Daemon. He wanted to not distract either of them. But there was a touch of belief.

"You should not have come here," Julian told her. "This is *my* home. Those are *my* family."

"The king is not real." She shook her head violently. Denial in every movement.

"He is and you are on the wrong side of history."

Fear and anger made men dangerous, but they made Vampires *very* dangerous. Julian's expression was *murderous*. And that cut through her defenses. She knew something was wrong here. Julian shouldn't have been able to take out Gerard. He shouldn't be this strong. And his *eyes*... they weren't right. She decided to bolt, seeking cover in the crowded high streets.

Julian, speed and strength are not your only powers. She is going to flee. Stop her. But not with your body. With your mind. See if you can, Daemon suggested.

She did a backflip that would have taken her over to the neighboring roof, but Julian *reached* for her and she hung suspended in mid-air. She let out a gasp and Julian nearly dropped her, but caught her again. Sweat stood out on his fledgling's forehead as Julian used telekinesis, gift of the Ashyr Bloodline.

Pull her back onto the roof, Daemon ordered.

Shaking and with more sweat pouring down his face, Julian dragged her back inch by painful inch. But it was beautiful to watch. His fledgling was amazing.

I'll handle it from here, Daemon said. *We need to greet your guests.*

From below, Liz said brightly, "Ah, I've found the keys!"

They had no idea what had happened up here. Daemon used the Eyros gift to send Gerard and Celeste into a sleep that only he could wake them from. He then dumped Celeste unceremoniously down beside Gerard like two sacks of garbage.

Julian was still shaking and sweating when he turned towards Daemon. His fangs were out and he was rubbing his temples, trying to calm down, but not succeeding. Daemon embraced him with one arm while he lightly brushed his fingers across Julian's forehead. His fledgling let out a sigh of relief and dropped his hands from his head. His fangs retreated, too.

"What did you do to me?" Julian asked, but then waved off an explanation as he heard Liz fussing with the front door. "Forget it. We need–"

Daemon lifted them both off the room and landed them behind the Thornes on the walkway without Liz or Henry being any the wiser. He then gently patted Julian's ass to urge the young man forward to address them.

"Liz! Henry! What are you two doing here?" Julian sounded

strained and a little breathless, but he doubted that the Thornes would notice, as they would be too grateful to have found one of their little flock.

Both Thornes whipped around to face them in surprise. Henry Thorne had his son's blond hair though that had turned an ashen color and thinned slightly, giving him a widow's peak with age. Intense gray eyes regarded Julian and Daemon. He did not see Daemon's red eyes though. Neither of them would notice them at all. Liz Thorne's hair was also an ashen blonde and there was a touch of her son's elfin features in her face. Her dark blue eyes widened.

"Oh, Julian! There you are! You're okay!" She flew down the few steps to him and wrapped Julian in a desperate, motherly embrace.

Julian hugged her back, a little stunned by her worry. "Of course, I am. Why were you worried?"

"Honey, I *watch* your show! You and Christian promised something big this week, which can only mean one thing," she said, kissing the side of his head and pulling back to give him a loving, but firm look. "Vampires."

"Oh!" Julian squeaked and swallowed.

"And I know it's foolish, but since your parents... well, since your parents' deaths, I've always worried that you and Christian might follow them too far," she admitted. "And then you weren't answering your phones and I really got concerned. Blame mother's intuition, but I just was worried."

"You're a believer in Vampires then?" Daemon asked quietly. He stood a few feet away from them, arms crossed at his wrists behind his back.

"I--oh, Julian, who is your friend?"

He admired the fact that Liz Thorne did *not* let go of Julian when she finally, truly noticed him. Instead, her hands tightened on his fledgling, a boy she thought of as her son as much as she did Christian. She sensed that Daemon was dangerous, or perhaps, she was just naturally suspicious of any men who were interested in one of her boys.

"Ah, Liz and Henry, this is–is Daemon." Julian paused awkwardly. "We're... we're... we're dating."

Dating? That sounds so mild for what we are doing, what we are, Daemon sent to Julian telepathically.

Well, I can't very well tell her that you're my Master! I think she'd be a little more unnerved than she already is, Julian replied wryly.

Why not? They'll have to be told sometime. Unless you believe Christian wants to cut all ties with them or use mind control on them so they never notice you do not age?

No! God, no! Julian was horrified and couldn't imagine either future. *But Christian has to be the one that tells them, if he is going to.*

Indeed. So we must keep them in the dark for now, Julian.

Henry stepped over to Daemon. He was friendlier than his wife, but he wasn't exactly trusting either. He extended a hand, which Daemon took in a firm handshake. Henry's hands were soft, the hands of a scholar, but he wasn't weak. Those intense eyes were fixed on him. Henry was trying to figure out things about him from his clothes to his affect.

He flicked through Henry's thoughts on him and got: *Rich, definitely. The clothes say that. Older than Julian. Maybe a little too old. Smooth as well. Polished. Most definitely. Slippery? No, but he hides things. Secretive. Accent? Sounds almost English. I get a sense of nobility about him. I must look into him further for Julian's sake.*

"A little cold for being out without a jacket, Daemon, eh?" Henry asked out loud.

"Oh, Julian, you don't have a coat on either! What are you up to running around like this?" Liz tutted as she embraced Julian to keep him warm.

"We were just, uhm, coming from the car to the house," Julian said.

"Where's your car?" Henry frowned as he looked along the street.

"In the garage," Julian quickly said.

"But you're coming in the front way?" Liz cocked her head to the side. He read from her mind that the garage was out back.

His fledgling was terrible at lying to these people at least and the pathetic, puppyish looks he was giving Daemon almost had the Vampire King laughing.

"Why do we not go inside?" Daemon gestured towards the front door where Liz's keys still hung out of the keyhole. "Julian has told me so much about you."

Liz gave out a high laugh that contained a sort of sharpness though, too. "Well, he hasn't told us about you, Daemon... ah, what is your last name?"

"King," Daemon said smoothly. "Daemon King."

"Well, I look forward to hearing all about you, Mr. King," she said.

"Daemon, please."

"All right. And as Julian said, I'm Liz and you've shaken hands with Henry."

"Pleasure. After you, please." Daemon tipped his head towards the door.

Julian's eyebrows rose and sent telepathically, *You're good at this.*

Reading people's minds has its perks. And I have more experience with people than you.

But not humans, right?

Not these modern humans, but people are people. You'll see. The trappings might be different. Cars instead of horses. Cell phones instead of letters marked with wax seals. But people are people.

The four of them moved there as one. Julian was the one to use the keys, wiggling it a little in the lock before turning it. The bolt slid home and Julian turned the knob and pushed it open. He flicked on the light in the warm and inviting foyer. The illumination came from a simple chandelier that hung over a maple-floored space.

Julian let the three of them precede him into the house before he hurried ahead of them to turn on more lights. Daemon slowly allowed himself to take in the space that was very much Julian's home.

Wingate, he savored the house's name. It suited the home somehow.

He followed after everyone down an arched, tall hallway that led to the back of the house. On the walls were framed photographs of

Julian's parents in exotic locales. They were always smiling. Their expressions somehow intimated that they were always meant to be together, even in those rare shots where they might not be touching. A young Julian with a gap-toothed grin often stood between them, parents' hands on his shoulders. It was clear that the three of them had been a tight unit. Three people who had genuinely loved one another, but perhaps more importantly, had *liked* one another.

Julian took them to a kitchen. Though it was far from the fire pits that he had seen in the past with these sleek metal containers–*appliances,* Julian's mind corrected him–and rich stone counters, he could still recognize this room for what it was. A place where human food was prepared. There was even a fireplace fitted with a spit along one wall. A wave of regret filled Julian at that moment as he realized there was nothing in this room–other than the Thornes, from whom he would never feed from–that was edible. Julian's exertions had burned through his slender reserves. Daemon would have to feed him very soon.

Julian settled himself at the kitchen island and gestured for the others to do the same. "Would you guys like something to eat or drink?"

"I wouldn't object to some wine," Liz said. "Henry and I were just at that bistro you boys told us about. Most divine French onion soup and steak frites, but I find that I always want more wine after eating something so richly delicious."

"No problem. Henry?" Julian lifted a wine glass that was a delicately blown crystal cup on top of a thin stem.

"I wouldn't mind," Henry said with a smile.

Julian got out two glasses and was opening a bottle of red wine when Liz frowned and asked, "Aren't you two having any?"

Julian's eyes went immediately to Daemon before his mind voice asked, *Are we? Can we?*

Of course, we can.

"I would adore some wine." Daemon was curious if the fermenting technology had improved since he'd imbibed some of the sour yet refreshing vintages the humans had made in Nightvallen.

"I'll get more glasses. You open that bottle so it has a chance to sip the air!" Liz laughed and she got two more of the delicate wine glasses down from a glass-fronted cabinet and set them on the counter.

Julian poured out the ruby red liquid that was made from fermented grapes. Unlike the vintages he had experienced, this one seemed far richer and more fragrant. Julian slid a glass to Daemon after the Thornes had been served. He took a sip. The complexity of the drink totally absorbed him for a moment.

"It's very good, isn't it?" Liz asked him.

"Quite complex," he said.

He took another swallow. Part of him just wanted to drink this wine and do nothing else until he had unlocked all of its secrets, but the Thornes had to be put at ease.

Julian was awkwardly spinning his glass. He took a sip of wine, but the taste was not blood and young Vampires were often too overwhelmed by their newly heightened senses to partake in other food.

"So how did you and Julian meet, Daemon?" Liz asked.

Julian choked on his wine. Henry had to pound his back while Liz rubbed his nearest shoulder.

"Sorry," Julian got out. "Went down the wrong pipe."

"I hate when that happens," Liz commiserated.

"Julian and I met over our common interest in Vampires," Daemon said once Liz and Henry were looking at him again.

"Oh?" Liz did not look happy. She took a large swallow of her wine and her fingers clenched that slender stem too tightly.

"Are you a professor of some kind?" Henry asked.

Daemon knew Henry would be investigating him the moment he had a chance so lying too overtly wasn't a good idea. Julian wouldn't want him to use mind control on them if he didn't need to. So Daemon shook his head.

He had not established an identity here. He had understood that much from Balthazar that Vampires took on human personas and had written documents and a "cover" on Earth. Daemon did not yet have such things. He wasn't sure if he wished them. Or would he reveal the truth to humans once he re-established his rule over Vampire-kind as he had in the past?

"I am just a dilettante. I found Julian through his show." Those were the right words. Julian and Christian were actors of some kind. He did not quite understand Julian's explanation about Youtube and content creators. "We corresponded and then met."

"I see. And are you of the opinion that Vampires are real, Daemon?" Liz asked.

He knew from her thoughts that he would fall farther in her estimation if he said he did believe, because she thought Julian's obsession with Vampires was unhealthy. If he believed, he would be driving that obsession in her opinion. But if he lied and told her no, then when the truth came out, which it would, she would never quite trust him again to be truthful with her when it counted.

"I do," he said simply.

Julian coughed again. Henry pounded his back.

"On what basis is this belief centered?" Henry asked dryly.

"Guys, let's not do this, okay? I believe in Vampires, too and–" Julian began.

"It's all right, Julian. Other than yourself, I think I am right in saying that the Thornes have understandable concerns about the type of person who believes in Vampires," Daemon interrupted.

"You don't have to undergo the Spanish Inquisition though," Julian muttered and his gaze flickered between the two Thornes, unhappy with the lying, but more unhappy with their pressing of Daemon.

They have no reason to trust me. In fact, Julian, they have every reason not to. They sense that I am a predator. They sense that you are quite fond of me. They are right to be concerned, Daemon assured him telepathically.

"I base it on the very simple fact that belief in Vampires has existed throughout all recorded history. Every culture has their version of immortal, bloodsucking beings," Daemon answered.

"But surely, you know that werewolves and Vampires were used as ways to explain aberrant behavior in humans," Henry pointed out.

"Here is the thing about that theory, you can believe that all of humanity was too simple, stupid or superstitious to understand the world, or you can accept that they were recording exactly what they saw and it was the truth. They had experiences with beings who were immortal and fed on human blood," Daemon answered.

"But there are many beliefs that our ancestors had that were nonsense!" Henry argued. "They believed the Earth was flat and that the sun revolved around the Earth. They believed disease came from foul air. On and on it goes!"

"True." Daemon nodded his head. "But you also agree that there are things that *you* believe to be true now, which will later be proven to be false, correct?"

Liz swirled her wine in her glass. She looked half amused and half dismayed. "And you think that our belief that Vampires aren't real will be one of those things?"

Daemon took a large sip of wine and his eyes met Julian's. "Yes."

"Well, I look forward to being proven wrong then." Henry lifted his glass. "Speaking of looking forward to something. Where is Christian?"

Again, Julian looked at him in alarm. "Uhm, he's..."

"With the person he's dating," Daemon said smoothly.

Liz's mouth dropped open for a moment in utter surprise. "*Christian* is dating someone, too, that he hasn't told me about either?!"

"Ah, well, he..."

"It's new," Daemon answered for his floundering fledgling.

Liz put one hand on her hip. "Well, I think a dinner party is in order to get to know Daemon better and what is even the name of this man Christian is dating?"

"Balthazar. Balthazar Ravenscroft," Julian got out.

"Say that name three times fast." Henry lifted an eyebrow.

Daemon grinned. "Just wait until you meet him."

Seeing Balthazar "meeting the parents" was going to be perfect. Eyros had always been fascinated with new people. He enjoyed talking with them and finding out every single thing they thought.

"Good, then we'll set it up." Liz took out her phone and went to what she thought of as her "calendar".

Julian shrugged and tried to say nonchalantly, "Maybe in a month-
-"

"This week," she corrected.

Julian blinked. "W-wait? What?"

She looked up at Julian and said with definitiveness, "Tomorrow or the next day will be best for Henry and I. You and Christian choose which one of those two dates will work. No excuses."

The Story Continues in Volume 3!

Made in United States
Troutdale, OR
06/08/2025